Prairie Schooner

Book Prize in Fiction

EDITOR Hilda Raz

Carrying the Torch

Brock Clarke *Stories*

University of Nebraska Press

LINCOLN AND LONDON

Acknowledgments for
previously published
material appear on page xi.
© 2005 by the Board of
Regents of the University of
Nebraska. All rights reserved
Manufactured in the United
States of America ⊛

Library of Congress Cataloging-in-Publication Data
Clarke, Brock.
Carrying the torch / Brock Clarke.
p. cm. — (Prairie schooner book prize in
fiction)
ISBN-13: 978-0-8032-1551-1 (cloth : alk. paper)
ISBN-10: 0-8023-1551-7 (cloth : alk. paper)
1. Southern States—Social life and customs—
Fiction. 2. Northeastern States—Social life
and customs—Fiction. I. Title. II. Series.
PS3603.l37C37 2005   2004029038

Set in Scala by Keystone Typesetting, Inc.
Designed by A. Shahan.
Printed by Thomson-Shore, Inc.

for Quinn

And it is possible that he lost his head, and that he was carried away by his ideas. This was because he was no mere dreamer but one of those dreamer-doers, a guy with a program. And when I say that he lost his head, what I mean is not that his judgment abandoned him but that his enthusiasms and his visions swept him far out. ≉ **Saul Bellow**

Contents

Acknowledgments

The stories in this book have appeared or are forthcoming in the following magazines and anthologies:

"Carrying the Torch," *New England Review*
"For Those of Us Who Need Such Things," *Georgia Review*; *New Stories from the South, Best of 2003*
"The Reason Was Us," *Georgia Review*
"The Apology," *New England Review*; *Pushcart Prize xxix: Best of the Small Presses, 2004*
"The Ghosts We Love," *Virginia Quarterly Review*
"The Son's Point of View," *Southern Review*
"Geronimo," *Greensboro Review*; *Stories from the Blue Moon Café iii*
"The Fund-Raiser's Dance Card," *Southern Review*
"The Hotel Utica," *Five Points*

Thanks to the University of Cincinnati, the Taft Fund, and the Bread Loaf, Sewanee, and Wesleyan Writers' Conferences for their generous financial support of this collection.

Thanks to the editors of the magazines in which these stories first appeared, especially T. R. Hummer, James Olney, Stephen Donadio, and Jodee Rubins.

Thanks to the good people at the University of Nebraska Press for all their hard work on my behalf.

Thanks to Michael Griffith, Keith Morris, and Elizabeth Sheinkman for their advice and friendship.

Finally, thanks beyond thanks to my family—Lane, Quinn, Peter, Elaine, Colin, and Alonzo Clarke—for whom I'm so grateful and to whom I owe so much.

Carrying the Torch

Carrying the Torch

I decided last night that someday soon I am going to rip my husband's penis off with my bare hands. I plan to do it while he's sleeping. I will make sure that I am wearing my running shorts and sneakers, and after I have done the deed, I will jog at a good clip around my neighborhood, holding the bloody thing above my head and a little in front of me like a torch. The summer Olympics started yesterday, and I was in the crowd as Rafer Johnson ran through Atlanta with the real torch, which is how I got my idea.

"Who exactly is Rafer Johnson?" I asked my husband, Till, yesterday. Till is an executive with Microsoft's Atlanta division, and he's also on the Olympic organizing committee, which is how we managed to stand right up front while this large, fit black man ran down Peachtree with *Nike* written all over his mesh tank top and nylon jogging shorts.

"Rafer Johnson needs no introduction," Till said. He sounded offended that I had even asked him such an ignorant question. Then Till started paging through his official opening ceremonies program. I don't think he knew who Rafer Johnson was, either.

"I'm sorry I asked."

"Apology accepted."

"Let me see that program," I said. I found Rafer Johnson's biography immediately. "It says here he was a decathlete."

"I knew that," Till said.

Then, while I was reading about Rafer Johnson's illustrious Olympic career, Till excused himself.

"I have to see a man about a horse," Till said, which I know now meant that he had to go find this lady vice president from Coca-Cola with whom he is having an affair. This is not the first time this kind of thing has happened. I don't even want to count the number of times Till has run roughshod over our marital vows. His flings have become so routine, he doesn't even bother apologizing anymore. Which is another reason why I want to do what I want to do.

But I didn't know about the lady vice president at this point yesterday. I thought Till was just going to get a drink or use the facilities.

"Go and find your horse," I told Till.

This he did. Till went into the organizing committee hospitality tent and found and then rode his soft drink executive horse, while I stood there watching Rafer-Johnson-who-needs-no-introduction sweat underneath all the TV lights. While I was watching, two guys in red blazers stepped out into the middle of Peachtree and put the brakes on Rafer Johnson's forward progress. They told him there was a glitch up ahead. The news didn't seem to affect Rafer Johnson much. He just shrugged and ran in place to stay loose. The two guys in blazers, however, seemed very concerned about the reper-cussions of the holdup in general, and about Rafer Johnson's pro-fuse sweating in particular, maybe because of his proximity to the eternal flame. They told Rafer Johnson to cool his jets while they toweled him off.

I hung around for a while, waiting for Till to come back and watching these two men in loud red blazers towel Rafer Johnson off. I was standing right next to a cameraman for NBC, and so through his microphone I could hear the announcers making small talk and trying to kill time. They were talking about the New South and how Atlanta was the city that was too busy to hate and so on. While I was listening to them talk, some white guy next to me in a gray pin-striped business suit and a white *Atlanta 1996* baseball hat tapped me on the shoulder.

"Someone better call the police," he said, pointing at Rafer John-son, who was just starting to run again. "Some black guy is stealing the torch."

"That's not some black guy," I told him. "That's Rafer Johnson."

"Even so," the guy said.

I looked around to see if anyone had overheard this conversation that we were supposed to be too busy to have. No one had, but still. As the wife of an Olympic organizer, I decided that I didn't have to stand around and listen to this kind of stuff and be made to feel socially uncomfortable. We all have to make our stands. So I headed off toward the organizer's tent to find my husband. I found him in the back of the tent with the lady Coca-Cola executive, who was wearing a red business suit. They both looked spacey and smelled a little ripe and fruity, like chardonnay, even though they were both drinking scotch. I knew what this meant. I'm no idiot.

"Evie," Till said, "I'd like you to meet Sarah Jameson Fuller."

"Nice to meet you," Sarah Jameson Fuller said, sticking out her hand.

I ignored the hand. "So, is she the horse?" I said to Till, just like that.

"Excuse me?" the horse said.

"She is," Till said, just like that.

"The horse has three names," I said.

"She certainly does," Till said.

"*Excuse* me," the three-named horse said.

"I'm going home," I told Till. The three-named horse's hand was still out and so I shook it. Then I walked to the shuttle bus stop, where I waited in line for two hours for the shuttle to take me to my car. Once I finally got to my car, the traffic was so bad it took me two more hours to drive to our house in Marietta. It's normally a thirty-minute trip. By the time I hit our two-year-old faux Tudor on Sweet Briar Lane, I was steaming. If I were a big drinker, I'd have downed all of Till's pricey single-malt scotch. If Till and I had had children, I would have beaten them, or at least sent them to their rooms, immediately after I was done drinking that scotch.

Instead, I took a nice long bath.

I decided two hours later to do what I am going to do. I had gone to bed, and then gotten up to go to the bathroom. When I got out of the bathroom, Till was in our bed reading the *Journal-Constitution*. I didn't even hear him come in.

"I didn't even hear you come in."

"I took off my shoes. I didn't want to wake you."

"I was already awake."

"That's not my fault."

"It's *all* your fault," I told him. Then I mentioned some of the women I know he's slept with since we've been married: two co-workers, one cigar bar waitress, one woman who monitors the salad bar in the company cafeteria.

"I could go on," I said.

"We've hit a few bumps in the road," Till admitted.

"Don't forget Sarah Jameson Fuller," I said.

"Are you about done?" he asked, yawning.

"What I'm saying is that you are going to kill our marriage if you keep on with Sarah Jameson Fuller," I told him. "I'm serious. This is the last time."

Till nodded. "It's problematic," he said, just like that.

Then he turned off the light and went to sleep.

And that's when I remembered Rafer Johnson bearing the torch and, well, you know the plan.

I go into work this morning and talk up my big plan. I work thirty hours a week at the local computer supply warehouse. I'm not just speaking generically: the name of the place actually is Computer Supply Warehouse. I took the job three months ago so I could keep busy and stay in touch with the worlds of high technology and commerce, which Till said was necessary for my self-esteem. I told Till that at Hollins, where I went to college, I learned that the only things a girl needed for self-esteem were healthy interpersonal relationships and a nimble, nonlinear mind. Till said that Hollins was full of bull dykes who didn't know the difference between a douche bag and a Think Pad, and that they could kiss our yearly Alumni Fund contribution good-bye.

Till definitely gets not one bit of sympathy, is what I'm saying.

Steve, one of my coworkers, is the first person I see at work. Steve is my only friend at work, and I always tell him all about my marital troubles. Steve is also a big thinker who has just been accepted to the medical school at Emory, and so I figure I might pick his brain.

"How was the opening ceremony?" Steve asks.

"Life changing," I say. Then I tell him my plan. I don't leave anything out.

"With your bare hands?" he asks. I can tell he has doubts.

"Bad idea?" I ask.

"Let's brainstorm," Steve says.

We're a couple minutes from being officially open, and so there are no customers to bother us yet. Steve and I head to the back to the break room, where he has his *Gray's Anatomy* and his *Merck Manual of Medical Information*. He hands me the *Merck* and tells me to find what I can find. I start from the beginning, which is probably not the best idea. I don't get much beyond the medical terms and their components. I learn that *spondylomalacia* is a softening of the vertebrae. I learn that *cranioitis* is an inflammation of the skull. I learn that the medical world is full of information that is not going to help me with my particular problem.

Steve, however, has better luck. I know this because he starts making clucking sounds with his tongue and the roof of his mouth.

"What's the verdict?" I ask.

" 'The human body's appendages can be cut without difficulty, but they are not easily stretched or pulled apart or ripped from their fleshy moorings.' I'm reading straight from the text."

"Translate," I say.

"I think you're going to need some kind of machine," Steve says.

"I'd like to keep this simple," I say.

"I wonder if you could rent a winch?" Steve says.

Just then, the store manager, Bob Sassas, comes into the break room. Bob Sassas is just a kid, younger than either me or Steve, and he always wears official blue store oxfords that are much too big for him. Bob Sassas is also a brisk walker, and when he strides from printers over to computer games, it looks like he's in full sail.

When Bob Sassas sees us looking through Steve's medical dictionaries a full five minutes after opening time, he nearly hits the roof. Three other computer superstores have recently opened nearby, and so Bob Sassas has been a little tense about the suddenly crowded niche market and the store's endangered bottom line. His claps his hands together to get our attention and his shirt billows and flaps.

"What do you two think you're doing?" he asks us.

"Doing a little bit of research," Steve tells him.

Bob says he can see that. Bob also says that if we want to keep our meager salaries and our csw employee discounts, then we better take our big eggheads out of our books and go help our valued customers with their individual software needs.

After Bob Sassas leaves, Steve tells me that he's sorry he hasn't really helped me with my domestic situation. Steve also says that if medical school weren't so incredibly expensive, he would take one of our computer mouses and thread it through Bob Sassas's small intestines. I tell Steve that if this job weren't so important for my self-esteem, I'd help him.

We congratulate each other for our strong principles. Then, Steve and I take our big eggheads out of our books and go help our valued customers with their individual software needs.

Twelve hours later, I find myself standing over the body of my sleeping husband.

I spend a good deal of time positioning myself. I set my feet far apart and think about what kind of grip I might use. Till sleeps on his back, which theoretically makes my task a little easier. Theoretically, all I should have to do is plant my feet, yank, and hope for the best. But I quickly find out that theory has its limitations. Theory, for instance, doesn't help me ignore the moonlight coming in the window, lighting up my husband's smooth, still handsome face. Theory also doesn't help me ignore the memory of nine years ago, when Till and I first met. Till had just graduated from Vanderbilt and had just been hired by Microsoft. We went out for a drink one night and ended up on the tenth floor of the downtown apartment building where the company was putting Till up until he found a place of his own. I was a temp worker at Microsoft, just out of Hollins. Hollins had taught me that it was liberating and actually instructive to have casual sex with young men who had Old South pedigrees and New South business acumen. Till fit that description. So I had sex with him. But Hollins also taught me that it was unwise to become emotionally involved with these same young businessmen, because of their fake tans, unlimited expense accounts, and predatory approach to love. On the night I'm talking about, I watched Till sleep, just like he's sleeping now. The moonlight poured in the window, highlighting Till's tan. He didn't look predatory. He looked like Adonis, or someone like that. Hollins didn't really teach us anything about the Greeks.

So I decided to ignore Hollins. After all, what the hell did Hollins know about moonlight?

Now, nine years later, I stand over Till's sleeping body and suffer a sudden loss of nerve. I decide that the conditions aren't right, what with the strong moonlight and the even stronger memory of first romance. I decide to put off doing what I'm going to do until tomorrow, definitely tomorrow.

I go downstairs and sleep on the couch. I wake up with a jagged crease on my forehead from sleeping on the cushion zipper. The jagged crease is bad enough that I can't completely cover it up with makeup. Till notices the mark on my forehead immediately when he comes downstairs for breakfast.

"Morning, Frankenstein," he says.

"Did I ever actually love you?" I ask.

"You're awfully touchy," he says.

This general pattern repeats itself for about a week. During the days, Till and I go to work. We do not speak to each other at the breakfast table, nor do we call each other on the phone. Till gets home around nine after a stopover, he tells me, at the Olympic Village. We do not speak much then, either. I watch television and Till reads the paper or maybe a business periodical until about ten o'clock. Then he goes to bed. He doesn't even bother saying good-night. I don't know whether he's kept on with Sarah Jameson Fuller and I don't care, because the damage has been done and I am determined to do what I am going to do.

But I don't do anything. Each night, I watch the Olympics until eleven or so. Then I go upstairs. I stand over Till's sleeping body with my legs far apart for balance and freeze up, wondering about why people lose love and whether they can ever get it back. You see, I can't completely forget that Till wasn't always this awful a husband. On Monday, an Iranian male gymnast gets the bronze in the floor exercises, and I think of how at our wedding Till read a Kahlil Gibran poem just because I asked him to. On Tuesday, a German wins the shot put, and I think of how Till and I once went to an Octoberfest in Walhalla, South Carolina, where Till sang "Deutsch-land Deutschland Über Alles" until the organizers said they would give him a porcelain beer stein if he would just shut up, which he did. So they gave Till a stein, which he presented to me with a great sweeping bow. He was very romantic. You can't just completely for-get small gestures like that. And on Wednesday, a skinny British girl elbows an older Italian runner to the ground during the women's ten thousand meters. The older runner rolls over onto the infield and lies on her back, reaching her arms out dramatically toward the sky, screaming something in Italian. The British girl feels so bad about the incident, she doesn't even finish the race; instead she runs back to the fallen Italian, telling the woman she didn't mean it and begging for forgiveness. I watch all this and think about how Till felt so guilty about his first fling—with Sheryl in the Microsoft travel division—that he confessed without me even confronting him, without me even knowing anything at all about Sheryl in travel. I remember how Till wouldn't stop apologizing, wouldn't even let go of my hand until I said I would forgive him, which I did. Till promised that it was the last time and that I wouldn't regret it.

Then, on Thursday, I watch an American decathlete pull a ham-string during the hundred-meter hurdles. The decathlete sits right on the track, weeping, pounding his fists on the track's surface. The announcers explain this is the third time he's hurt himself in as many Olympics.

"What did I do to deserve this?" the decathlete asks rhetorically during the post-race interview. "I stretched before the race, I swear."

"You don't deserve it," I shout at the TV. "There's nothing you could have done."

"You could always coach high school," the interviewer says.

"You're right," the wounded decathlete says. "I've run out of chances."

Afterward, I go upstairs, stand above Till, and silently cry over our own lost opportunities.

Today, Friday, I decide not to watch the Olympics at all. As a result, I don't think about the past. Instead, I stand over my sleeping husband and think of how my friend Steve is probably right, that I won't physically be able to tear Till's penis off with my bare hands, and how embarrassing that will be.

While I'm thinking about all this, Till wakes up and sees me standing over him.

"What do you think you're doing?" he asks me.

I tell him.

"With your bare hands?"

I nod.

"Not too likely," Till says. Then he goes back to sleep. He doesn't even bother rolling over. I feel worse than the Kenyan who missed the steeplechase because of an attack of colitis. They announced his condition right on the TV and everything.

"Are you still there?" Till asks a few minutes later. This time he doesn't even open his eyes.

"I am."

"Are you sleeping on the couch again tonight?"

"You're damn straight I am."

"Can you shut the door when you leave? Last night you forgot."

"Don't push me, Till," I tell him, lowering my voice into a growl.

"Just whenever you leave."

I growl at Till a little more. Then I shut the door, go downstairs, and sleep on the couch.

All evidence aside, I am not the crazy one here. After all, I have my reasons for doing what I want to do. What are Till's reasons? Do I not look as good as I did nine years ago? Do I not spend three hours a day at the gym? My aerobics instructor says I have the body of an eighteen year old. I set the gym record for consecutive hours on the StairMaster. Do you think Sarah Jameson Fuller holds any kind of exercise machine record at her club? My personal fitness expert told me that all men want women with good legs and challenging workout regimens. Is this not what men want after all? Has Till changed the rules of male-female attraction without telling me? Does he have one good reason for becoming so bad? Should he not get what's coming to him?

It is Saturday night. Till is upstairs in bed. I am downstairs, telling myself all this stuff in an attempt to get up the courage to try one last time to exact my wifely revenge. Meanwhile, on TV, they are showing some Yugoslavian sculptor in war-torn Sarajevo who is building a miniature version of their Olympic stadium out of concrete. The concrete, the sculptor says, is from the remains of the 1984 Olympic stadium, which has been blown to hell by one of the many warring ethnic factions. But it doesn't matter that the real stadium has been destroyed, the sculptor says.

"Symbol," the sculptor says, "more powerful than real thing."

Right on, I think.

Inspired, I shut off the television and go to the basement, where Till has his woodshop. I am down in the basement all night, designing and making a wooden facsimile of Till's severed penis.

Till gets up around eight in the morning. He can probably hear the saw noises coming from the basement, and so he opens the door that leads from our kitchen to the basement to see what I'm up to.

"What are you doing down there?"

"I'm making a wooden facsimile of your severed penis," I tell him.

This gets his attention. Till comes down the stairs and looks at the block of wood on the jigsaw table.

"That's a little small, isn't it?" he says. Then he goes back upstairs to make some coffee. A little while later, I hear the front door slam and the car pull out of the driveway.

But Till is right. It *is* a little small, especially if I want my neighbors to positively identify the facsimile and what it represents while I'm running around the neighborhood, holding it like a torch. So I scrap the version I'm working on and get myself a much bigger block of pine.

I am supposed to work at the Computer Supply Warehouse at eleven, but I'm so involved with my project that I decide to call in sick. I get Steve on the phone.

"I'm not coming in today," I tell Steve.

"How goes the emasculation?" he asks.

"It's moved from the literal to the figurative." Then I tell Steve about the Yugoslavian sculptor and my change in plans. To emphasize my newfound commitment, I hold the receiver down to the jigsaw and do a little detail work.

"What do you think?" I ask Steve after I've picked up the receiver again.

"You might need professional help, Evie," he says. Steve definitely sounds disturbed, which I did not expect. "Why the change in tactics?" he asks.

I say that there are a number of reasons. I mention the high quality of Till's Black & Decker jigsaw and my long-standing interest in arts and crafts. I mention that when I look out the window at our subdivision, I see nothing but cul-de-sacs, identical three-bedroom, two-bath starter homes, and state-of-the-art automatic sprinkler systems, and that I want to make something beautiful to add to this stale, ugly world. I mention my weeklong experiment in hopelessness, standing over Till, knowing that I will not be able to do what I want to do. I mention my hopelessness during the nine years of our relationship, give or take a few genuinely reciprocal magic moments. I mention that Till was the first person at Microsoft Atlanta to make vice president before he was thirty; I tell Steve that I want to be the first at something, too, and that I bet no one has ever done what I'm about to do. Finally, I mention to Steve that over the last nine years I have never, not once, finished what I have started; I tell Steve that Till always finishes what he starts.

"This is why I've changed my plans," I tell Steve, revving the jigsaw. "I'm doing it because I know I can. I know I can finish the job."

Steve says he's impressed with my stick-to-itiveness, and that he's being paged in software and has to go. He sounds more disturbed than ever. I ask Steve if he's okay. Steve says No, he's not okay, that I'm scaring him just a little bit.

"Tell me we're still friends," I say to Steve.

"I don't think we are," Steve says. "You don't need me as a friend anymore. That's what scares me."

I tell Steve that he is a worse coward than the Bulgarian weight lifter who disqualified himself because of a little quadriceps twinge during the clean and jerk.

"Guilty," Steve says. Then he hangs up.

This makes me sad at first—losing a friend like Steve, who I find out wasn't that good of a friend in the first place. Then I realize that this is the kind of risk I take, stepping so far outside the mainstream of woodworking and domestic violence.

So long, Steve, I say to the phone receiver.

Welcome to your new world, Evie, I say to myself.

After my conversation with Steve, I work twice as hard on my project. I go right through lunch and dinner, scrapping perfectly adequate finished products that don't live up to my suddenly high standards. When I finish with the actual woodwork, I apply some flesh-colored paint, and then some blazing red paint the approximate color of blood. By the time I am through, I am holding an oversized but still reasonable facsimile of my husband's severed penis.

I go upstairs to wash my hands and change into my running clothes. While I'm changing, I call our neighbors. I tell them that in fifteen minutes they should be standing out in their driveways if they don't want to miss something they might never see again. Unfortunately, it turns out that I have a little competition. My neighbors inform me that a bomb went off in the Olympic Park earlier this morning and that they're busy watching the TV coverage and might have to take a rain check. Luckily, I have a response for this unexpected news. I tell my neighbors that if they would consult their Olympic history, they would find that the 1972 games in Munich were disrupted by a similar act of terrorism, and, sad as it is to say, they can reasonably expect it to happen again in the future, too.

"But what I'm about to do," I tell Mrs. Calhoun from down the street, "may be a once-in-a-lifetime experience."

"Like Haley's Comet," Mrs. Calhoun says.

"Exactly," I say.

"Honey, I'll be there."

"Don't forget to turn your porch light on," I tell her.

I have finished my phone calls and I am doing my calf stretches when I hear Till pull in the driveway. When I go downstairs, Till is in the basement, staring at you-know-what.

"Welcome home," I say.

"You really did it," he says. His voice sounds like Steve's did, like I'm teaching him something he didn't think was even out there to be learned. And in the first time since I don't know when, Till has a look of real regret on his face. It is difficult to tell whether it is a regret of the "Baby, I should have loved you better" variety, or of the "Jesus, I should have called the police when I had a chance" variety. But still, it's something. I stand there a while, watching his face twitch and gray a little. The transformation is very satisfying.

Unfortunately, we stand there for so long that my calf muscles begin to lose something of their looseness. So I grab my facsimile and start to head upstairs.

"Evie, wait," Till says.

"What?" I say.

"Why?" he asks.

This question is not as easy to answer as you might think, and I stand at the foot of the stairs for one more minute, considering my response. I could tell Till what I told Steve: that I'm doing it because I actually can, because I want to be the first at something. I could tell Till that extreme injustices call for extreme forms of protest. I could tell Till that I've made what I've made because it is disposable, and once I am done parading around the neighborhood I will throw it away, effectively ending our marriage. Or I could tell Till that in one last effort to find our lost romance, I will jog around the neighborhood so quickly and so furiously that I will achieve something like a time travel, and when I am done with my run it will be nine years earlier and all of Till's and my bad history will be erased and there won't be any Sarah Jameson Fullers or white bread Marietta subdivisions or wooden facsimiles of my husband's severed body parts, just Till sleeping in the moonlight and me watching him.

But I don't say any of this. How do I say something like this and not feel a sadness that I shouldn't have to feel? How do I say something like this and then take what should be my triumphant victory lap?

So I ask Till if he wouldn't mind repeating the question.

"Why?" he asks again. I think I can see his regret dissolve just a little, which reminds me of where we are and what I am here for.

"Symbol," I say, "more powerful than real thing."

Then, before I lose my nerve, I climb the stairs up from the basement into the kitchen, and then walk out the front door. I can see our neighbors standing in their driveways, waiting for they-don't-know-what. They've turned on their porch lights like I've asked and their automatic sprinkler systems are on, too, the water arcing and dancing in the 60-watt lights. For once, the world looks beautiful, and before it changes, I take a big, courage-building breath, raise my symbolic torch above my head, and begin my run up and down Sweet Briar Lane, not knowing how long I will run or what my run will change, knowing only that I am finally first at something.

For Those of Us Who
Need Such Things

I was driving through Savannah, Georgia, and discovered that the city was deserted, agreeably so, and so I made some inquires and one thing led to another and I ended up buying the whole city, cheap. Of course, the city fathers had to sign off on the deal first. They were suspicious of my motives and asked: "Are you one of those fellows who buys up abandoned cities, remakes them into sanitized versions of their former, authentic selves, and then sells them off at a huge profit?"

"Oh, no, not me," I said, because I had heard of these men, had read about them in all the major magazines, and it gave me a little bit of revulsion, what they did to perfectly good, deserted cities like Santa Fe, New Mexico, and Monterey, California, and Charleston, South Carolina, the way they hired people from the suburbs and had them move to the city and pretend to be genuine adobe-dwelling Pueblo Indians or authentic downtrodden cannery workers or fourth-generation Gullah basket weavers. "Not my style at all," I said to the city fathers.

"So why in the world would you want to own a whole city?" they asked.

"It's complicated," I said.

"Try us," they said. It was clear that the city fathers weren't going to finalize the sale of the city until I told them the whole story. So I sighed and told them the whole story: of how my wife had just left me and moved back to upstate New York, where her parents lived, because of certain personality conflicts that had caused us to grow apart after three years of marriage. And one of those personality conflicts that had caused us to grow apart was that I had cheated on her, once, with her best friend, and then lied about it, and my wife happened to be the kind of upstanding person who needed to be able to trust her best friend and her husband, and she was also the kind of upstanding person who hated cheaters and liars. Even so, it was an amicable breakup, so amicable that it became clear that I was losing a wonderful, singular woman who had such extremely high moral standards that, if you were a cheater and a liar, she wouldn't give you one more chance even if you begged her. It pained me to know that I would never find another woman like my wife again, and it also pained me to sit around our house in Jacksonville, Florida, which was so cramped with regret and despair that I couldn't think straight. So I decided to find a bigger place, a place like Savannah, where I could be by myself with my few worldly possessions and contemplate how I had ruined my marriage and how I might someday set things right again.

The city fathers sat there quietly and listened to my story. When I was done, they asked: "You mean you've got yourself a broken heart, don't you?"

"Yes, I suppose so."

"Well god*damn*, why didn't you just come out and *say* so?" they said, because the city fathers were highly sympathetic toward broken hearts, having themselves been divorced by wonderful women for cheating and lying. We all got teary and agreed how difficult it was to live in the cruel, cruel world, and then we talked about the weather for a few minutes, and then the city fathers stood up, smoothed out their khaki pants, hitched up their belts, signed over the city to me, got into their Lincoln Town Cars, and drove back to their duplex condominiums and their youngish second wives in Tybee Island, just outside the city.

So that was that. I moved my stuff and myself into an enormous pink brick house off Bull Street. For a long time, I simply walked around Savannah and surveyed my new property. Even though it was run-down and mostly abandoned, it was still a very pretty city, with all its nice parks and waving palm trees and sagging wrought iron balconies and that good, rotten salt smell blowing in off the water and all that spooky, dying sunlight filtered through the Spanish moss. Yes, it was a fine southern city I'd purchased, an excellent place to be by yourself and contemplate your broken heart and store your few worldly possessions.

But then I got lonely, as will happen to owners and sole inhabitants of decent-sized American cities, so lonely that I called my wife at her parents' house in upstate New York. I told her how I'd been living in monastic solitude in my new city, how I'd been thinking hard about what I'd done to her and how I'd broken her heart and mine, and how the solitude had been good for me. Except that now I was lonely.

My wife, if she were a certain kind of person, might have said how lonely it had made her to see me and her best friend, drunk and pawing each other at our annual Labor Day barbecue, and how lonely it had also made her feel when her best friend and I had feebly denied that anything "funny" had gone on between us, even though we were standing there with our clothes half off. But instead she said: "If you're so lonely, you should join a club." This was constructive advice, and not at all mean spirited. So I said to myself: "What kind of club would be appropriate for my fine southern city?" Because I didn't want to go off half-cocked and form just any club to ease my loneliness: sure, I wanted a group of people with whom I could share my city, but I also wanted the right kind of people, the kind of people who wouldn't be too out of place and ruin all the good salt smell and wrought iron. So after some careful consideration, I went out to the western suburbs, hired twenty overeducated old ladies, set them up in the abandoned movie house, and asked them to start a literary society. In doing this, I was not at all like that man who bought Omaha, Nebraska, and ordered that the paved roads be made into dirt roads and ordered that all men wear denim overalls and that all women wear calico dresses and that livestock be herded through the dirt streets 24/7, and that Omaha be referred to on all promotional materials as the Original Cowtown,

U.S.A. No, I hired the old ladies because I'd never been to a southern city that didn't have a literary society run by overeducated old ladies, and because it seemed appropriate for me, as the owner of the city, to be concerned about the city's cultural life. Besides, my wife had always been something of a patron of the arts and for many years had been a season ticket holder for the Jacksonville Philharmonic. I wanted her to approve of my choice in clubs and see that I was someone who deserved a second chance, because it occurred to me now that my city wasn't just a place to contemplate my sins, but also to atone for those sins by making the city into something better than it was and thus make me look better in the bargain.

Anyway, the whole thing was slow going at first, because it took the ladies some time to apply for the appropriate federal grants and write their manifesto and to organize their first symposium on the future of southern literature. But I was careful to stay out of ladies' way and not to meddle too much or micromanage in any way. Soon enough the grant money started rolling in and the symposium definitely answered all the relevant questions. It was a great comfort, believe me, to smell the cigarette smoke wafting up from the street to my bedroom window after the symposium concluded, and to hear all the voices agreeing with each other as the symposium contributors walked away into the inky night.

But the old ladies didn't stop there. Encouraged by the success of the symposium, they began to hold regular Monday night poetry readings. They were nice enough to ask me to attend the inaugural reading as their guest of honor. It was the first poetry reading I'd ever attended. I can't describe the feeling of walking out of the dank, salty air and hearing a professor from the local college reading a poem about that dank, salty air, and then walking back out into that very same air after the reading: well, it's enough to make you feel real again. And when people from the audience came up to me after the reading and said: "This is a fine little city you've got here," I agreed with them and felt very lucky indeed. This was what I told my wife on the phone afterward: how lucky I felt to own such a fine city with such a fine literary society, and yet how strange it was to feel so blessed and to miss her so much at the same time and to have such mixed feelings about things. My wife, if she were a certain kind of person, might have mentioned the mixed feelings she had when her best friend and I tried to excuse our cheating and lying by saying: "We were drunk" and "It didn't mean anything." Instead, my wife said kindly, patiently: "You just went to a poetry reading, so why don't you write a poem about all your mixed feelings?"

And I would have written a poem, I really would have, but right after I talked to my wife Thanksgiving hit, and the literary ladies got hungry, and we had a problem, because I wasn't much of a cook.

"What is it you want to eat?" I asked them.

They said, "We wouldn't mind some collard greens and a mess of sweet potatoes and maybe a nice deep-fried turkey since it's Thanksgiving and everything."

"Okay," I said. My first thought was to hire a caterer, but there's something very distasteful about caterers, something temporary and mercenary and nomadic about them, and I didn't want something like that polluting my nice little city. So I went out to the northern suburbs, met with several black women who jointly owned a chain of soul food restaurants, and explained my situation to them.

"What do you want us to do about it?" they asked.

"I'd like you to open up one of your restaurants in my city."

"So those white ladies got something to eat," they said, deadpan-like.

I said, "I know, I know." I told them I appreciated the long, troubled history of such a relationship, and I insisted that I wasn't insensitive to how offensive my proposal might seem to them, and I made it clear that I was all too aware of the intersections between race and commerce and the imbalance of political power in our supposed democracy, and I stated and restated my sympathies until they said: "We'll do it if you'll shut up. Plus, we want to bring our husbands."

So we had a deal. The women opened a restaurant on Abercorn Street and brought their husbands with them. I was nervous at first, not just for the obvious reasons of race relations, but because I was concerned with my nice, empty city becoming too crowded for a man to think about his broken heart and do penance for his sins and maybe even win back the affections of his estranged wife. Then there were the husbands, who couldn't cook and had nothing at all to do with the restaurant. I frankly wondered how they were going to occupy themselves.

But I needn't have worried, because it turns out that the husbands were good men, very engaged men who, as it happens, were involved in neighborhood politics and who were also involved in community theater. These were not men to sit idly for too long, and one day, soon after their wives opened the restaurant, the husbands came to me with a proposal. They reasoned that if their wives were there to make the old literary society ladies feel comfortable, then it was only fair that the husbands be allowed to make the old literary society ladies feel uncomfortable.

"What do you have in mind?" I asked.

They said: "We want to sit on the park benches right outside the restaurant and wear heavy, tattered clothes, even in the hottest weather, and drink forty-ouncers out of paper bags."

"Paper bags," I repeated, thinking about it, letting the idea soak in.

"Except they won't really be forty-ouncers," the men explained, "they'll be Coca-Colas, but they'll be in paper bags, and when the old white ladies walk by, we'll feign inebriation and harass them."

"Will you cackle at them incomprehensibly?" I asked, because I'm not afraid of a little innovation now and then, and because these men were very good at setting the scene. I could envision the whole thing already.

"We might," the men said. "But wouldn't it be better if we hurled fake voodoo curses at them?"

I agreed that it would be better, and so they made it happen, and it ended up being a wonderful piece of guerilla theater. The white women complained about the black men to the black women, and the black women, who knew all about their husbands' plans, complained theatrically about the men to the white women and went outside and said "Shoo" to the men, who stayed put. Then the black women went back inside the restaurant and everybody ate their turkey and their collard greens and complained a little more. One of the black women was so wise and artful in her complaining that the white women suggested that she write some of the complaining down in a book. The black woman said: "Already did that," and then handed the literary ladies a manuscript, which was a collection of the woman's life lessons and recipes entitled "In the Kitchen." The manuscript was a complete surprise to all of us. Before anyone could catch their breath, the literary society named the woman its first writer-in-residence and there were hugs all around. The husbands even came in the restaurant to hug their wives and managed to do so without breaking character and soon the emotions were running so high that everyone got completely exhausted and had to call it a day. Somehow all of it was both genuine and ironic, which, as I told my wife on the phone that night, is all you can ask for in a modern city, which is something those hucksters who buy abandoned cities, etc. never seem to be able to understand: that you can't just hire fifty Salvadoran migrant workers and set them up in state-of-the-art Ogunquit roundhouses off the pedestrian mall in downtown Portland, Maine, and have the concessions people sell Coca-Cola out of calcified squash gourds and try to pass the whole thing off as the real deal without the least bit of self-consciousness and then expect the Salvadoran Ogunquits and the paying customers and everyone else not to feel horribly empty after a while.

"You've got to be honest, even when you're dishonest," I told my wife, not even trying to hide my double meaning; which is to say, not trying to hide the fact that I when I spoke of the Ogunquit roundhouses I was really talking about the way my lying and cheating had derailed our marriage and how I'd never, ever do anything like that again. Because this is not the same world it once was, and if you hurt your wife you can't just go out and buy her flowers and expect her to forgive you, you've got to do something dramatic, like buy a city and do something real with it and distinguish yourself from those other men who buy up abandoned cities for the wrong reasons, and once you've done all this, you have to apologize for breaking your wife's heart and you have to do so both directly and through analogy. "You've got to be honest, even when you're dishonest," I repeated.

"That's true," my wife said in a wistful faraway voice that seemed plenty promising to me.

"I've got something really special going here," I told her. "You'd be proud of me and my city."

"I think I would," my wife said, and she didn't even tell me to write a poem about how proud I thought she'd be of me and my city before she hung up.

Well, it was quite a beginning for me, the owner of Savannah, and I had high hopes that my wife would continue to see what a sea change I'd undergone vis-à-vis my city and soon she'd move to Savannah and we'd reconcile and run the city as equal partners. This was exactly what I was thinking when the former city fathers came in to Savannah one day, saw what I had done with the city, and wanted to be involved somehow in the city's "renaissance," which is what they called it. I understood what they were saying, completely. Who could blame them for wanting to live in a real place again after dying a slow death in the gated condos and planned communities out in Tybee Island? And I would have been happy to include them, honestly, except that they had gone out and done some reading and all they would talk about was about rebuilding the city's infrastructure and how we needed to improve the city's bond rating and so on. Understandably, I didn't want this kind of boring, officious stuff coming out of the mouths of my city's fathers, because it's very difficult to ease your wife's broken heart and your own when people are spouting figures and acting fiscally responsible. So I told the former city fathers "No thanks," and sent them back to Tybee Island.

I should have left it at that; I know this now. But I was still thinking about how my running of the city seemed to have changed my wife's mind about me, somewhat, and I was also thinking about the black men and their fake forty-ouncers and fake voodoo curses, how cutting edge their work was and how their guerilla theater had made the city innovative and authentic at the same time. I was inspired, maybe too much so. In any case, instead of leaving well enough alone, I went out to some of the suburban golf courses and found eight colorfully dressed, overweight sixty-year-old men who would only talk in sports metaphors and didn't give one shit about going through the proper channels or due process, and who were not averse to making wild, sometimes nonsensical, sometimes offensive public proclamations, and I hired them on the spot to be my new city fathers.

Once their salaries were agreed upon, I gave the new city fathers offices in city hall and I also gave them an endless supply of Early Times bourbon and a team of press agents who taught them to always speak in the infamous misdirectional southern doublespeak we hear so often on television, which, at the time, seemed like a nice little flourish on my part. Sure, my city was a bit more cluttered than I would have liked it, but the city fathers and their oversized personalities made the place more true to life, it was undeniable. And if the new city fathers said a couple of things that sent some of the black women into fits of quiet rage and the black men into heavier fake drinking and the overeducated white ladies into making fierce *tsking* sounds while they read their poems during open mic night, well that was true to life, too. Besides, I made sure everyone was well compensated for their work.

"Don't worry about a thing," I told my wife on the phone. "It's all under control."

"Are you sure you aren't overdoing it a little bit?" she asked.

"You sound like you're worried about me," I said hopefully.

"I *am* worried about you," she said. "Maybe you should stop and take a deep breath or something."

"Okay," I said, and told my wife how touched I was that she was thinking of me. I swore to her that I'd stop and take a deep breath or something.

But then the old men came back to town, the old widowed white men who had moved out to the lower-middle-class suburbs in the 1970s, and I didn't have time to take a deep breath. The old men, whose wives had all recently died, took note of the white literary ladies and the black women and men and the outrageous, corrupt city fathers, and they got sentimental over how the city used to be, before they abandoned it for their brick ranches and fenced-in back lots. These old men began to trickle back to the city—first as visitors, then buying the assisted living condos I'd built in the old warehouses on River Street. This was nice, and I welcomed it at first. For one, it's expensive to own and run your own city, and I was happy to get some cash flowing in via the condo sales. For another, it was certainly nice to see the emaciated old widowed men sitting on the benches in the public squares with their legs crossed and dangling at the knee, chain smoking Winstons as they no doubt used to do back in the days of old.

But the thing is, old people, as a rule, are on tight budgets and thus prefer to sit on a free public bench and *look* at things and not buy anything, not even styrofoam cups of sweet tea to go. This freeloading upset the black women, who were not making any money from the old men; and it upset the black men, who had grown used to having the benches as their own private stage; and it upset me because the old men looked so lonely and sad and so *near death* that they made me think of my wife, so far away in upstate New York, and how sad and lonely I really was in my heart of hearts and how I was afraid I'd never win her back and what it would be like to die all alone some day. My mood was grim, is what I'm saying, so very grim that one day, just before Christmas, I asked one of the old men if he could at least pick up a banjo and play it while he was sitting there, just to add something to the ambiance of my nice little city. I said: "Maybe you could play something high and lonesome and transcendent, a tune by Ralph Stanley or Bill Monroe or the yodeling Jimmie Rodgers, that kind of thing."

Well, when I suggested this the old man stared at me for about a half hour before going back to crossing his legs and not getting his banjo and not playing a Jimmie Rodgers song and not buying anything, either.

It was at this point, three months after I had purchased Savannah, that I learned a valuable lesson: you cannot feel good about your city if you have too many old people living in it. So first, I instructed the city fathers to put a cap on the number of retirees allowed to live in the city at one time. This caused some grumbling from the condo dwellers and bench sitters, and it also caused some grumbling from the city fathers, who accused me of being Machiavellian and exactly like those men who we all read about, those men who buy up abandoned cities and sanitize them to hell and then sell them off at a huge profit. This was a sore spot with me, as I've mentioned, and the accusation almost made me rescind my cap on the elderly population. But in the end I didn't and in the end the city fathers did what I told them to, because, as I pointed out to them, it was my city and I could do whatever the hell I wanted with it.

"You actually said that?" my wife asked when I told her about the old men and my showdown with the city fathers.

"I sure did."

"You're sounding a little weird," she said. "A little out of control. You don't sound like yourself at all." And if I had listened carefully, I would have heard what my wife was really saying, which was simply this: "Remember that deep breath I told you to take? Will you please just stop what you're doing and take a deep breath?" But instead, I heard what I wanted to hear, which was: "I'm proud of you, the way you're working so hard. Keep working hard, the more the city changes the more you change, so keep proving yourself to be a different man—almost all is forgiven."

"No time to talk," I said, because I was inspired by what I thought I had heard, and because I was late for an emergency meeting with the old literary ladies and the black women and black men. I had called the meeting so I could ask them what we could do to make the city a little less depressing, a little more lively. To a person, they said we needed more young adults.

"Are you sure?" I asked them.

"Adults aged twenty-one to thirty have more disposable income and dine out ten times as often as people in the next highest age bracket," the black women said, reading directly from a government study.

"They don't sit on benches, either," the black men said. "Those benches are our stage. Without a stage, we've got no theater."

"Yes," the old ladies said, and they also said how young they felt at heart and how just the sight of the old bench-sitting men was bringing them down in a big way.

"Okay," I said. That very afternoon I got in my car, drove to Atlanta, assembled a focus group of men and women aged twenty-one to thirty and asked them what it would take for them to move to a nice little southern city like the one I owned.

"We'd like to see Irish pubs and deep dish pizza joints," the focus group told me, in unison.

I thought perhaps I'd been misunderstood. So I repeated the question.

The focus group said, "We'd like to see authentic Irish pubs with trivia games on Wednesday night and folk singers on Thursday and pizza joints specializing in deep dish pizza."

This presented something of a problem, understandably, because it was my city and I had gotten plenty attached to it and so I didn't want to ruin it with any kind of quick fix. Besides, I wasn't sure that Irish pubs or deep dish pizza places were the kind of thing the old literary ladies or the black women or their husbands had in mind, and they had all helped so much in easing my broken heart that I didn't want to betray their trust. And then, in the back of my mind, I thought of those men we all have heard about and loathe, the men who buy up the abandoned cities and turn them into theme parks and manipulate tourists and residents alike with their bogus notions of authenticity, and then resell the cities at a huge profit. I didn't want to be like them, it was true: but were Irish pubs and deep dish pizza joints something these developers would be interested in or not? On the one hand, the developers might not think Irish pubs and pizza joints were authentic looking enough, which would be reason enough alone to allow them in my city. But on the other hand, were these developers so concerned with the bottom line that they would do anything to make a profit? It was confusing in the extreme, and I called my wife to get her opinion on the matter, but she was out, running errands. Without my wife's guidance I had to rely on my own instincts, and my instincts looked around and saw the old skinflints loitering themselves into slow, certain death on the benches and bringing the whole city down with them and depressing the hell out of me, the guy who owned the city *and* its benches, and my instincts said: "All right, let's do it."

So I did it: I made the necessary contacts and hired the appropriate restaurateurs and beer distributors and converted some of the assisted living condos on River Street to singles pads and in general made way for this infusion of youth that my fine little city so badly needed. And it worked, in a sense: before I knew it my city was invaded by armies of young men dressed in Duck Head khakis and young women dressed in tight pastel T-shirts, all of them chewing gum and drinking beer at the pubs and then eating pizza after the pubs closed and then on the way home singing out the fight songs from whatever universities they'd just graduated from with degrees in accounting and industrial management. And while I didn't exactly appreciate the young men and women puking in the public squares after the bars closed, and while I quickly got sick and tired of the Irish folk singers belting out "Margaritaville" in the pubs five times a night, and while I loathed the way my new young citizens referred to me as the "mayor guy," and while I became near homicidal every time the kids insisted I yell "I *own* that shit" whenever they would name a building or statue or anything else that fell within the city limits of Savannah, it was true the city was full of something—*life* maybe—that it hadn't been so full of before, and it was also true, in terms of population growth and cash flow, that my Irish pub and deep dish pizza experiment worked out extremely well.

In another sense, though, it turned out disastrously, as I found one morning when I woke up and discovered that my house was being picketed—the old literary ladies, the black men and women, the college professors who read their poetry at the literary society, the old bench sitters, all of them holding signs and walking in circles in front of my nice pink house, all of them irate over my Irish pubs and deep dish pizza joints. The black women were seething over the pizza joints, which were taking away some of their business; the black men were upset that there were too many kids walking around with plastic cups full of beer from the pubs, which lessened the shock effect of their fake forty-ouncers; the literary ladies and professors insisted that it was impossible to write poems about the dark, forbidding night and the whispering palm trees and the haunted hallowed ground with all this pizza and beer and youthful exuberance to contend with; and the old bench sitters pointed out that many of the kids who washed dishes and glasses at the pubs and pizza joints were also skateboarders who used the benches for ramps and whatnot and made freeloading almost impossible and potentially life-threatening. Then, once everyone had had their say, a memo was read from the city fathers, saying that their mood was blacker than a Bantu in a coal mine and that I'd hired them to be city fathers of a southern city and that if Irish pubs and pizza places were southern then they didn't know what and that as history and football showed you could knock a man into the dirt and you could make him eat the dirt but you couldn't make him like it.

"Listen," I said from my front stoop. "This was your idea. I did this because of you."

"We hate you," they said.

"Go to hell," I said, because I'd absolutely *had* it by this point. After all, here I had been, interviewing people in Atlanta and hiring contractors and worrying about the literary ladies and the black men and women and *busting my ass* all over the place, and yet I wasn't enjoying myself or my city one bit. "Go to hell," I said again.

"We thought you'd say something like that," one of the literary ladies said. With that, the picketers all turned heel and marched toward city hall. If I'd been thinking clearly, I would have been concerned about this march in the extreme. But I wasn't thinking clearly, I was too busy thinking how hard I'd worked and how unappreciated I was and how I deserved the chance to let my hair down a little for once. So I went back inside and let my hair down a little for once, which is to say I drank Early Times bourbon straight out of the bottle until I passed out, and didn't wake up until the next morning.

When I woke up the next morning the damage had been done and I'd more or less lost my city, but I didn't know it yet. In fact, I felt good, real good, because the sun was bouncing off the wrought iron just so and the thick sea air was seeping in through the window and Bull Street was absolutely quiet. The city felt properly spooky and real again, like it was when I bought it, and I was once more proud to be its owner. I was feeling so generous I even allowed myself to regret some of the things I'd said to the picketers the day before.

With this regret in mind, I went straight to the city hall and my city fathers, thinking that I would have to make up with them before I got the rest of my city in order.

The city fathers were all sitting in the conference room when I arrived.

"We've got to talk," I told them.

"You *know* we do, boy," they said.

I didn't like this "boy" stuff, and I also didn't like the way they were looking at me, angry-like and eyes squinty.

"What's going on here?" I asked.

"You've made a mess of this place," the city fathers said. "So we got ourselves some outside help."

I didn't like the sound of this, either, but before I could say anything else, a man in the corner of the room, a man I hadn't noticed when I first walked in, stood up and walked to the podium at the head of the conference room. The man was young—in his early thirties maybe—with expensive casual khaki trousers and a white knit polo shirt. He was so handsome he made your teeth hurt.

"Don't even tell me," I said, because I knew exactly who this man was: he was the most famous man among those men we've all heard about, the man who had bought up Times Square and kicked out the real prostitutes and drug dealers and hired all of Epcot Center's most experienced employees to be fake prostitutes and drug dealers and instructed them to offer the tourists blow jobs and rock cocaine but to do so in such a way that wouldn't make the tourists uncomfortable and to also do so in such a way that parents could turn the whole thing into a cautionary learning experience for their children, if they so desired.

"Listen," I told the man right off. "I'm not sure if you know this, but this is my city, I own it, and it's not for sale. Besides, you're not exactly welcome here."

"That's not what *these* crackers told me," he said, hooking a thumb in the direction of my city fathers. The city fathers seemed taken aback by this remark, and I was encouraged for a moment, because I had grown up in Florida and so I myself had a healthy amount of regional resentment. I thought, perhaps, the man's comments would turn the city fathers against him. But it was strange: the more the man insulted the city fathers, the more he put them on the defensive and thus the more at ease they seemed to be. Before I knew it, the city fathers were making a number of familiar, sly jokes about the man being a carpetbagger and this being the second wave of Reconstruction; and then the man made some familiar, aggressive jokes about the city fathers' social backwardness and the ruinously high fat content of their food. Soon they were getting along like fraternity brothers.

"Hold on a minute," I said. "I still own this city."

"Shouldn't we let the people decide who owns the city?" the man asked. "Isn't this a democracy?" It was a clever question, I'll give him that, because I couldn't very well come out and say, "No, it's not a democracy," and still be perceived as the kind of city owner I wanted to be. So I reluctantly agreed to call a town meeting to let the people decide who they wanted to own their city.

The town meeting was held that very afternoon. The man spoke first. He argued that he sympathized with the citizens, that he had worked with many, many cities and so he knew what it was like for a city and its people to go through this kind of identity crisis. He added that if he were allowed the privilege of buying up the city, it would still be in a very real sense *their* city, and he knew they wanted their city to be an authentic southern city, didn't they? They did, obviously, because there was much clapping and whistling.

"Super," the man said, and then explained that he'd done some research and found out some interesting things. Did the citizens know, for instance, that the Irish had been among the first residents of Savannah, and so the Irish pubs—*my* Irish pubs—were both genuinely Irish and genuinely southern and didn't that make the citizens feel better? It did, obviously, and so did the man's plans to hold an annual St. Patrick's Day parade, during which the pubs would serve free green beer courtesy of Budweiser, with which he had some sort of connection. More clapping, more whistling, a smattering of encouraging hoots.

"But what about those damn pizza joints?" someone in the crowd asked.

"Not to worry," the man said, and he explained that as part of his research he learned that as long as the pizza joints were operated and staffed by citizens of Georgia, then they could be considered authentic, too. "I looked it up," he said.

A huge wave of relief passed over the audience. The more the developing man spoke the happier my citizens got, and the more discouraged I became—not because my citizens hated me, but because they had forgotten me so quickly and so completely. I over-heard some of the college professors telling the literary ladies that perhaps they had underestimated the tragic, lyrical qualities of youthful exuberance. The old literary ladies said they would organize a symposium on that very subject, pronto. Everyone seemed to have a renewed sense of purpose. I even saw the old widowers smile grimly and clap their hands a little. Indeed, it seemed that the black women and men were the only people who weren't appeased by the man who had bought up Times Square and who was about to buy my city, too.

"What about our restaurant?" the black women asked.

"What about our benches?" the black men asked.

The man simply shrugged his shoulders and held out his hands, as if to say: "What can you do?" And when the black women and men stormed out, vowing never to return, the man bugged his eyes out in mock horror and everyone laughed. It was all disheartening, so very disheartening that I forfeited my turn at the microphone. And so the meeting broke up and everyone went home satisfied, until it was just me and the man. He had all the proper documents in his briefcase and he took them out, laid them on the table, and handed me a pen.

"Well," he said.

"Is it usually this easy?" I asked.

"Yes," he said, not gloating, just telling the truth. And so, without saying another word, I sold him the city of Savannah, and I was so saddened by the whole thing, I sold him the city for less money than I had paid for it in the first place.

After I was done selling the city, I went back to my house, called my wife, and told her everything that had happened. Because I had it in my mind that we were still in love, despite everything, and so I had high hopes that even though I'd failed to save my city from the kind of man who we all hate, I thought that maybe I'd done enough to ease my wife's broken heart and win back her trust.

So I told her the whole story, how I'd lost the city, etc. When I was done, she said: "I'm so sorry, I really am, I know how much this meant to you."

"It doesn't matter. You mean more to me than this city ever did," I said, really pouring it on and desperate.

"Oh," she said.

"Will you take me back?" I said, and I got down on my knees, even though we were on the phone and she couldn't see me.

"I'm sorry," my wife said. She really was sorry: I knew this because she started crying. But before I could say anything else she hung up, leaving me all alone, on my knees in a house that I didn't own anymore, in a city in which nothing was mine except for the broken heart and the few worldly possessions I'd come there with in the first place.

I assumed that would be the last time I would ever hear from my wife, and so, in the absolute pit of despair, I went about packing up my house, getting ready to move to someplace—I hadn't yet figured out where yet.

Then, a few days after our last phone call, my wife called.

"Listen," she said. "What are you going to do now?"

I told her I didn't know. "Why?"

"Because," she said, and then explained that two paper mills had just closed down in her hometown, Little Falls, way up there in upstate New York.

"Yes?" I said, hopeful, and yet afraid to be too much so.

"The workers don't know what to do with themselves: they're walking around town like zombies, giving the people who still have jobs the creeps."

"Yes?" I said.

She said, "So the city is looking for a consultant. Someone who can show the guys what it is they're supposed to do: someone to help them buy flannel shirts and grow out their beards and develop a taste for Utica Club beer and drink it all day in bars that don't make money and should close but never will and generally stay out of people's way. That kind of thing. I thought of you, obviously."

"Do you want me to take it?" I asked.

"I do."

"Does this mean you still love me after all?"

"I don't love you," she said, and then sighed. "I could never love you again after what you did to me."

"Well Jesus," I said, getting less hopeful and more angry. "Then why do you want me to come up there?"

"We won't be in love," she said. "But at least we could pretend."

"*Pretend*?" I said.

"It's better than nothing," she said. "Is it not?"

"I'll get back to you," I said, and then hung up. My first thought was to say: No way, because there was something extremely demeaning about my wife's proposal; because it seemed to me that it was, in fact, worse to pretend to be in love than not to be in love at all. It was the principle of the thing. This was exactly what I was going to tell my wife when I called her back; "I was going to say: "No way," and then, when she asked why, I was going to say: "It's the principle of the thing."

So why then did I call her back and say, "Okay, I'll do it"? Why did I leave Savannah—which I hear is now full of tourist trolleys and guided voodoo tours and stores on the Riverwalk that only sell products featuring peaches and pecans—why did I leave Savannah with a light heart and no ill will? Why do my wife and I now say, "I love you," each night before we go to bed even though we know better? And why don't we feel so horribly bad about doing so?

Because the world has changed, I've said it before, and you can't just buy a three-hundred-year-old city and expect it to be real, anymore than you can cheat on your wife and expect her to truly love you again. And if you can't have real cities and true love, then you settle for the next best thing. This is why I moved to upstate New York and this is why I'm happy enough to live out my life and pretend to be in love, and this is why I sit down on a daily basis with the laid-off mill workers and help them buy the proper clothes and drink the proper beer and feel the right kind of desperation and act the way they're expected to act, and this is why I will continue to work hard to create a world that looks true and real for those of us who need such things.

The Reason Was Us

I t was the spring of parties—of housewarming parties and birthday parties and Derby Day parties and Memorial Day parties and desperate last-minute Sunday parties where the host warns the children of his guests to stay off his newly laid grass seed and where thirty-five-year-old women smoke the cigarettes they were supposed to have quit and no longer really enjoy except for the secrecy involved in smoking them in the shady, far-flung corner of the yard and where grown men drink too much beer again and make big, elaborate efforts to take up the long-forgotten games of their youth—and it was also the spring when Martin Prunty moved next door and began breaking into our house.

This was in Shady Oaks, South Carolina. It was a Saturday in late March when Martin moved to the neighborhood. My wife, Lily, was out back with a wheelbarrow and a gardening book, trying to figure out which plant needed how much light. Our sons were in the front yard, menacing palmetto bugs with sharpened sticks. Me, I was drinking gin and watching Martin and his movers from our front bay window. Martin's house, like our house, like all the houses in Shady Oaks, was a brand-new colonial with blinding white siding and replacement windows with the stickers still on them and an attached garage so oversized it could have been its own house. I scrutinized Martin as one will a new neighbor: with a mixture of distaste and fear and elevated expectation. It was true, for instance, that Martin looked nice enough: his face was red and hale; his hair was black and short on the top, distinguished and flecked gray on the sides; his clothes—pleated khaki shorts, green and red polo shirt, slightly broken-in running shoes—were properly understated in middle America; he had a gut, but it did not hang like a sack over his belt, nor did he seem inclined to rub it; he talked with the movers as they hauled his furniture into the house, but he didn't seem to order them around or get under their feet or on their nerves. Other than the movers Martin was by himself, but I noticed the movers carting in a crib and a child's bed, and this made me happy, because as mentioned we had two kids and naturally hoped their new neighbor would have children, too. All of this caused me to regard Martin with some goodwill and high hope. On the other hand, it was also true that the moving truck was not part of a fleet from some well-known national company, and was not really a truck, either, more of a dirty white, elongated van. There was no lettering on the van indicating its origin or ownership, nothing at all except for the fading kelly green words "We Move U." Martin's house was at the very arc of the cul-de-sac, a position that seemed to suggest something about the prominence of its inhabitants, but the van's legend gave me not a sense of royalty but rather of mental retardation. The furniture didn't seem unusually shabby or secondhand, but there wasn't much of it, certainly not enough to fill the new house. When the movers were finished and the van pulled away, Martin got in his car. The car looked decent enough, but when Martin tried to start it the engine coughed and stuttered but would not turn over. Martin beat his head on the steering wheel a few times, then got out of his car and charged into his new house.

"Are you watching the neighbors move in?" Lily asked, coming up behind me.

"I am," I said, turning to face her. Lily's gardening book—*Soil for the Soul*—had hard-sold her on the restorative powers of plunging your hands in the loamy earth, except the author must have had black dirt in mind, not our red clay, because the fingers of Lily's yellow gardening gloves were blood colored. She looked like she'd just come from surgery.

"What do they look like?"

"Who?"

"Our neighbors."

"He looks nice," I said.

"He," Lily said. "Nice." She wiggled her red fingers at me as she walked away.

It should be said now that Lily and I had our share of problems, and like our neighbors, we had moved south to Shady Oaks to forget those problems. The Chisholms, for instance, who lived three doors down, had lived in Manchester, New Hampshire, until their five-year-old daughter died of liver cancer, and then they moved because they couldn't stand the thought of redecorating her room, driving past the park swing set she loved, walking by the neighbors whose names she mispronounced, pruning the trees she might have climbed. Lyle Heath, who lived next to the Chisholms, had run a dairy farm in Little Falls, New York, a farm with a perfect view of the Mohawk Valley, a farm that had been in his family for four generations and that, with the banks closing in, he had at last sold off to developers and quickly moved with his family to Shady Oaks so that he wouldn't have to see his barn torn down, his fences yanked up, the developer's prefab three bedrooms hauled in on flatbed trucks. And then there was Lily and me. I had cheated on her, I'm sorry to say, then begged her forgiveness, which she did not give, not exactly, not ever, really, just one day, a month after my confession—a month of crying jags and marathon silences and furious whispered truths—I came home from work and she said, "I'll bet South Carolina is nice. I'll bet it's easier to be married to a peckerwood there." So we moved to South Carolina. I got a job in admissions at Clemson University, and Lily and I spoke to each other very gently, very carefully, and we treated the past like the disposable object we wanted it to be, and Lily sunk her hands into the good red clay and I drank gin slowly, tiny sips at a time, and looked out our front bay window as if keeping watch for the inevitable advancing hordes, and when we weren't doing all of this, we went to our neighbors' parties.

That's when I saw Martin next: at Steve Yardley's April Fools' party. All of our neighbors' parties were themed. On Bastille Day at the Falvos' we were forced to wear berets, and Alexis Falvo drew thin mustaches with a black makeup pencil on all the men. On Derby Day at the Arnolds, the house was so full of people dressed like jockeys that it looked like a convention of lawn ornaments. But this was April Fools' Day, and I could already feel the smoldering hotfoots, smell the fake dog turds, hear the rude, happy tooting of the whoopee cushions.

Martin was there when we arrived, surrounded by our neighbors, who were talking effusively about the weather, the congeniality of the natives, the fact that we could and did leave our doors unlocked at night; they assured him that he would love Shady Oaks as they did. All of this was happening outside, on the paving stone patio. Martin's expression was somewhere between longing and panic, and in it I must have seen something of myself, because I went straight for the drink table, but Lily joined the throng around Martin. I could hear her talking about the flowering trees: "That's a hibiscus," she told Martin. "That's a crepe myrtle. That's a magnolia." Because Shady Oaks was a brand-new subdivision, these flowering trees were still young and runtish. Plus, the Yardleys sprayed them with something that made the leaves and flowers permanently glisten; they looked more like artificial plants than real trees, and Martin looked at them dubiously, as though they were part of the April Fools. But Lily persisted. "It's April!" she said. "In Buffalo" (we were from Buffalo), "there'd still be half a foot of snow on the ground now. That dirty kind of snow."

"Dirty snow," Martin repeated, the words guttural and from somewhere deep in his throat.

"That's a pink dogwood," Lily said. "Oh, you'll love it here."

"Sure I will," Martin said.

There were signs right away that he wouldn't, in fact, love it. Martin drank six beers during Kristen Yardley's twenty-minute harangue about the high quality of the local schools; he would not talk about his wife and daughters except to say that they were back in Acton, Massachusetts, and that he didn't know when they would be joining him; he was a quality control engineer for a tire and rubber plant down the road in Clemson, and when someone asked him what exactly a quality control engineer does, he laughed bitterly and said, "I change the world." And when Nina Stradling put a tack on Martin's chair—she was putting tacks on everyone's chairs—and Martin sat on it, he jumped up and screamed out, "Mother*fucker!*"

"April Fools," Nina said weakly.

"Ha!" Martin said. "Ha! *Ha!*" He grabbed a beer out of the cooler and left the party without saying good-bye.

After Martin was gone, we attempted to keep the faith, and Kristen Yardley told an elaborate false story about the time she was groped by one of the lesser Rolling Stones, but our credulity had abandoned us and no one had much energy for April Fools any more, and we all went home.

That night, after we'd put Eric and Peter to bed, and right before Lily and I went to sleep ourselves, I asked Lily what she thought of our new neighbor and she said, "He makes me sad."

"He wasn't so awful," I said.

"I was afraid you'd say that," Lily said. I rolled over on my side, but Lily didn't turn off the light, and I could feel her staring at me; if her eyes were laser beams, then the back of my skull would have been so much scorched bone and runaway brain matter. But I didn't roll over to face her, and finally she turned off the light and we went to sleep.

A few hours later, a noise from downstairs woke me. I lay there in bed, waiting for a second noise to confirm the first one. I listened and listened and I heard nothing else. It was three o'clock, that awful time between night and morning when you're either doing something you shouldn't or you're thinking about it, and I thought about the first time I'd cheated on Lily. It was with a coworker and friend, Amy Vincent, who was the same woman I'd then cheat with a dozen more times. We were standing outside the Northside Tavern in Buffalo, where we'd been drinking for an hour or two after work, talking that bright, reckless, brilliant talk of working people happy not to be at work any longer, and while I had never noticed

Amy's neck before—she might as well not have had one—at that moment it was angled just so, sleek and lovely in the unlovely streetlight, and I remembered being surprised to discover that in one second you could be one sort of man, and in the next you could be another. Then I heard another noise, a cough or a groan, coming from somewhere and suddenly Buffalo and Amy Vincent and her neck disappeared and I was back in Shady Oaks, in my house, the noise coming from downstairs, and so I decided to get out of bed and check the front door. When I did I saw Martin.

He was standing in the front entryway. The door was open behind him, and you could hear the bugs making their noises out there in the one plot of high grass and bamboo the developers hadn't sold off yet. Martin had on a bathrobe, even though it was hot out, and he still had his clothes on underneath the robe. His eyes were glassy, his face was a gray sheet, and it was impossible to tell whether he was asleep or awake. "Martin?" I said to him, softly. "Are you awake? Do you know where you are?"

"It hurts," he said. "Oh, it still fucking hurts," and then he turned around and walked out the door, closing it behind him.

For the most part I avoided Martin over the next week. This wasn't difficult. He went to work, and I went to work, and besides this was around the time when a university's first choices for next year's freshman class repel the university's advances, and so I was busy calling the waitlisted and telling them that they weren't losers, not at all, and that the Clemson University family loved them very, very much. Then there were the boys, who were having a hard time memorizing the pantheon of Civil War generals and battles as part of the school's local history curriculum, and so Lily and I spent hours tutoring them on the difference between Stuart and Lee and insisting that Sherman's March to the Sea was not an AIDS walk. And then there was Lily. She watched me; I knew this. I had done a horrible thing. I deserved to be watched. She watched me while I was doing dishes or playing catch with Peter or teaching Eric to tie his shoes; she watched me talk on the phone, after hours, to panicked parents of a prospective student about how much financial aid their child was or was not eligible for. Maybe Lily was looking for the me she once loved to banish the me she didn't; or maybe she was waiting for the me that had hurt her so to rear up again, so she could see that lousy me once and for all, commit me to memory, then leave me behind. I didn't want to give Lily anything to see; and I sure didn't want to talk about Martin, about him breaking into our house and me thinking about Amy Vincent, after months and months of not thinking about her.

But at dusk, when Lily was watering her garden (it was, *Soil for the Soul* said, the time of day when plants and humans were most open to replenishment) and the boys were playing their last, spastic round of whatever game they were playing before they went to bed, then I sat in my window and drank my gin and watched Martin's house. His family still hadn't arrived. Sometimes he wasn't around at all, sometimes you could hear him hammering or sawing in the backyard, sometimes he was sitting on his front porch, drinking his own drink. I wasn't haunted by him, not exactly, but I was looking for answers in him, the way Lily was looking for answers in me. Had he been awake or asleep that night he had broken into our house? Had he chosen our house for a reason, or could it have been anyone's house? And what hurt him so badly? But his face, his drinking, his hammering and sawing gave away no secrets.

I next saw Martin less than a week later, at the Ryersons' battle of Gettysburg party, which they held in mid-April and not on the February anniversary of the great battle because of some obscure theory that the battle *should* have taken place in April, and if it had then the outcome would have been entirely different. The Ryersons, it should go without saying, were Civil War nuts. In our invitations—scrolls of paper meant to resemble, I suppose, the one on which Lee had signed over the Lost Cause to Grant—we had been told to wear either blue or gray and Bill Ryerson occasionally fired a cap gun through a wet towel in imitation of some far-off rifle report and on the stereo there was martial music playing and on the television there was an endless Civil War documentary with the historians droning on about the bones of our dead boys and every now and then Beth Ryerson, who was wearing an antique gray dress with a ripped bodice (if the party theme was based in history, there was always a woman with a ripped bodice), walked around saying jokey, sexy things to the men about the condition of our weapons and whether we'd like her to unjam them.

In every other way, though, it was the same as every party I'd been to in Shady Oaks. We all drank, but reasonably, and the conversation stayed far away from the political or scatological or the seriously taboo and whenever the adult world of consequence and regret reared up and, for instance, someone started talking about a rock star's recent suicide around the Liddons, whose nineteen-year-old estranged gay son had hanged himself back in Allentown, we had the party's theme to retreat to, our safe haven where we did not have to think about the ways in which we'd hurt and been hurt, where we laughed about the sorriness of our costumes or praised the ingenuity of our hosts or debated, in the case of the Ryersons' party, whether or not smoked Gouda was actually ever served and consumed on a Civil War battlefield.

So it was the same party as always, except of course that Martin was there. He—like most of us—was dressed in Yankee blue: a light blue polo shirt and light blue pleated shorts and blue socks even and he looked very much like an oversized Catholic schoolboy in uniform. People regarded him warily. We'd all the seen the same movies, after all, the movies in which the menacing stranger comes to town and tears the community's fabric, etc. After Martin's performance at the Yardleys' April Fools' party, one couldn't be blamed for imagining that Martin would get drunk again and tell jokes he shouldn't or dance on the drink table or ogle the women in their ripped bodices or jump naked into the above-ground pool and generally rend us from the safety of our costumes and themes and be the overall bad wind that blew our doors shut and made us lock them behind us, which is precisely why we moved to Shady Oaks: so that we wouldn't have to lock our doors, so that we could forget that there might be a reason to lock them and that the reason was us.

Martin didn't do any of this. He didn't drink more than one commemorative plastic battle of Gettysburg tumbler of Kentucky Gentleman bourbon and laughed politely when people joked about Johnny Reb this and minié ball that, and was perfectly agreeable to his hosts—he didn't make any drunk driving jokes, for instance, which was good because Bill had once gotten tanked and plowed into the side of a school bus back in Cherry Hill, and a couple of the kids were in ICU for weeks because of it and he'd lost most of his family's deodorant soap fortune in the lawsuits that followed. No, Martin didn't say anything out of the ordinary and the party ended without incident of any kind. I even went up to talk to him right as the party was winding down. I could feel Lily's stare on my back as I extended my hand, introduced myself, apologized for not knocking a hello on his door and for being such a negligent neighbor.

"Don't fret," Martin said. "We have plenty of time to get to know each other."

"You should come over sometime, maybe some evening," I said. I waited to see a flicker of recognition, of guilt, of knowingness. But there was nothing. "For a drink or something," I said.

"I'd like that," he said. That was that. We shook hands and I went back home with Lily. Even Lily had to agree that Martin seemed perfectly fine, perfectly nice, and we fell asleep that night with our arms around each other, as in the days of old, me breathing through my nose as I'm prone to do, Lily smelling good, of the dirt she tilled and the soap she washed it off with.

It was three o'clock again when a noise woke me. I sat up in bed. Lily was still asleep; clearly she hadn't heard anything. It was a different noise this time—a banging of something hard on something hard—and it was clearly coming from inside the house. It was Martin of course, and of course I knew this, or suspected this, but I wasn't thinking of him: I was thinking of Amy Vincent. I was thinking of the hushed conversation we had the next day at work after we'd done what we'd done—first under that sickly yellow Buffalo streetlight, then in my car, then at her apartment. We both said how sorry we were, how very wrong it had been. "Poor Lily," Amy said, because they knew each other, had had several friendly conversations at Christmas parties and staff picnics.

"I know," I said.

"I know you love her," she said. "I know you love your kids."

"It's true," I said, because it was, and the fact that I hadn't acted like I loved them seemed worse to me at that moment than not loving them at all, not loving them ever.

"I'm not a bad person," she said, and I nodded, because she wasn't.

"So that's it," she said. It was a statement, not a question, and I agreed with her—we even shook hands on it—which was why neither of us could understand how we ended up in the same bar the next night, talking the same sharp, flirting I-dare-you talk; couldn't understand why we were then holding each other under the same sickly yellow streetlight; couldn't understand how, back at her apartment, we'd let ourselves do what we'd sworn not to do; couldn't understand the fear we felt as we lay in her bed, whether the fear had brought us together in the first place, or whether we'd made it ourselves. And now, more than a year later, I couldn't understand why I was thinking of all this as I was—with shame, sure, but also a little bit wistfully.

You can only think this kind of stuff for so long, and then you have to go confront the noise that made you think it in the first place. I got up, went downstairs. Martin wasn't in the entryway, so I walked down the hallway, into the kitchen. Martin was sitting at the table. The clunking noise had stopped, but there was a big red circle on his forehead, and so it was pretty clear that what I'd been hearing was skull banging on pine.

"Martin, do you know you're in my home, at my table?" I asked him. When he didn't answer me, I said, "Tell me what hurts, Martin. Does it still hurt?" He was still wearing his Union blue, again with a bathrobe over it; he had that same blank, gray look from the last time he'd broken into our house. It still wasn't clear whether he recognized me, whether he'd even heard or understood my questions.

"What is my problem?" he said. "What is wrong with me?" And once again, he got up and walked out the door.

Over the next month time became liquid and awful. One moment I was eating dinner with my family, awash in their good company and the slow dawning of Lily's forgiveness and the bounty of vegetables from her garden; the next, it was three in the morning and I could hear Martin banging around downstairs and I was remembering Amy, remembering what it felt like to touch someone new for the first time—which was about sex—and then to touch them a second or third or fourth time—which was about something else, something private and more complicated and terrible and closer to love. One moment, Lily and the boys and I were at the Palmetto Primary School play, grinning through the local fifth grade Annie screeching about her hard-knock life; the next, it was three in the morning again and Martin was moaning on the couch downstairs about his hurting heart and I was thinking about the time I'd crept into Peter and Eric's room after I'd come back from Amy's too late at night, how I said to them, very softly so as not to wake them, "Please, please save me." One moment it was Lily's birthday, her thirty-fourth, and I made her a cake, the frosting sugary enough to make your teeth scream and beg, and she kissed me on the cheek for the effort, right on the cheek, which you wouldn't think would be something more and better than a kiss on the mouth but was; and the next moment, it was three in the morning and Martin was on the enclosed patio, crying softly and asking, "Are you there? Oh, where in the hell are you?" Then, once he left, I got on the phone and called Amy Vincent. It was three o'clock in the morning back in Buffalo, too, and she wasn't happy to hear from me, but the lateness of the hour didn't have much to do with her unhappiness.

"I knew you'd call," she said.

"You were right," I whispered.

"Speak up," she said.

"I said, 'You were right.'"

"I wish I wasn't," she said. Amy was talking about the past, of course, and about how in it she told me she loved me, she did, and I told her I loved her, too, but that I'd that very morning confessed to Lily and promised her never, ever again and so things were likely to be impossible for a good long while and (and this is just one of the things I'm ashamed of) wouldn't Amy be happier applying for a transfer out of admissions, maybe into human resources or fundraising or some such friendly far flung division at the U of Buffalo? Good-bye was what she said then, and she was saying it now, too.

"Don't you ever think of me?" I asked.

"I'm not even thinking of you right now," she said, and then hung up.

The next morning Lily found me sitting at the kitchen table on which, weeks earlier, Martin had used his head as a mallet. Her birthday cake was in front of me, half eaten and wrapped in cellophane and, a day removed from its purpose and in the full morning light, looking not like something meant to be eaten but to be thrown away, and quick. Lily did just that, then walked back to the table and regarded me. I'm sure I looked how I felt—hollow and guilty and unclean—and she said, "I think I know you," and went out to her garden, which needed her.

There had been parties during these days and weeks, of course, and Martin had been breaking into our house only after one of the parties and at these parties I discovered that he'd been breaking in my neighbors' houses, too. Who knows what in the parties prompted Martin to do what he did, because at the parties themselves Martin was as dependable and good-natured a guest as there is on this watery globe. At the Liddons' May Day party, for instance, he dressed, like the rest of us, in a utilitarian denim getup that might have looked good on Chairman Mao. At the Greenes' Cinco de Mayo shindig, he pretended to understand Ricky Greene's gibberish fake Spanish, and took great pains to Olé! the Greenes' mutt, Lola—who was made up as a bull, with cardboard toilet paper innards for horns—whenever she ambled by. And at the Pattersons' Earth Day hoo-ha, he didn't complain when he drew the short straw and was made to dress as the sun, all in yellow, and stand stock-still as we—the party's earths, with our attendant greenhouse gases and ozone-depleting industrial fumes—swirled around him, Martin saying to us, "Is it hot enough for you?" and "How's your water table?" and "Is it hot enough for you yet?" as we orbited by.

So Martin hadn't done anything strange at the parties. Nonetheless, I knew he'd been breaking into my neighbors' houses in the middle of the night, too. I knew this not because they told me, but because their eyes were as dark and scooped out as mine, because those eyes followed Martin around at the parties, looking for clues as to what he knew and didn't know. What pains you so, Martin? we wanted to know. Who have you hurt, who has hurt you? Is it your family? Where are they? What have you done? What are you trying to tell us? How did we get so broken, Martin? And where can we find someone to fix us?

That Martin was haunting my neighbors, too, also became apparent in the parties' themes, which became something not to cling to but to distort, to stomp on and leave behind. For instance, at the Liddons' May Day party, Ted Liddon—whose son had been a male stripper before committing suicide—began taking off his clothes as we sang "The Internationale," getting all the way down to his yellowed jockey shorts before Cheryl, his wife, turned off the music and ushered him, weeping, into their bedroom. At the Cinco de Mayo party, Sasha Greene—who had a rage management problem, and who'd assaulted her elderly mother back in a Stamford nursing home—drank all the sangria, threw the dog's fake bull horns at her husband and then kicked the dog itself over and over, sending it howling out into the backyard. And speaking of backyards, on Earth Day, we smelled smoke, and so the whole party followed the smell outside and found Dave Patterson burning the normal party refuse—the paper plates and plastic utensils and the bottles and cans and even someone's kid's dirty diapers—in his backyard. Dave had been abused by a Catholic priest when he was a boy, and as the flames leapt and the acrid smoke poured heavenward, Dave was mumbling something that might have been a prayer, might have been an antiprayer. As if conjured by Dave's mumbling, Lily suddenly appeared across the fire from me. She looked like love, this was my exact thought. Because if love is not desire (which is what we're always told) or the best part of us (which is what we want to believe), then love must be the memory of love, and right then I remembered all the other times I'd seen Lily's face golden and flickering across bonfires and campfires and accidental grease fires on the stove and I loved her very much, and it seemed possible—likely even—that this was the last fire that I'd ever see her through. I nearly shouted out something stupid and desperate right then, something that would have come out of my mouth sounding like "Us! Us! We!" But I didn't and she didn't notice me standing there, or didn't want to; instead, Lily stared deep into the fire, stared silently, seriously, fatalistically, as if she were staring not at the ashes of the party but at the ashes of us.

The last party worth telling about was at the Bellinghams' and it had no theme. No theme! No costumes, no detailed invitations and instructions! There was no food, either. The Bellinghams only had cheap plastic handles of liquor and boxes of wine and case upon case of barely drinkable beer and bowls of cost-cutter cigarettes scattered everywhere. There was music playing somewhere, music that spoke directly to the hips and knees and the other parts that make up our lower halves. Lily saw a group of women standing in a circle across the lawn, smoking cigarettes, and even though she hadn't, to my knowledge, smoked a cigarette in a decade, she headed toward them, saying, "Good-bye, you," to me over her shoulder.

I drank one plastic tumbler of gin after another, wandered around in a daze. It was a real party, all right, the first one ever at Shady Oaks. Every few minutes someone tipped over backward in a chair. Lydia Olin was puking in the compost barrel; her husband, Thom, was pissing in the sandbox. Neighbors were dancing with neighbors, slowly, the way neighbors shouldn't; men without dance partners were singing unironically into half-empty beer bottles along with the song, a song no one had heard in years but was either everyone's favorite, or least favorite. Victoria Lyons was crying near the toolshed; she said she'd be all right in a second, but no one seemed to believe her. There was no pot, but there was a bong, and Miller Le Ray, the owner of the bong, insisted that you could get high on the resin, which wasn't, he insisted, more than two years old. Jack Bellingham had found an old croquet set in his garage, and he was arguing loudly with Tee Morrison about the Rules of the Game. Lawrence Milettti was swinging one of the mallets wildly, spraying the balls into thickets of feet and shins. Martin himself was holding a whole bottle of bourbon and staring balefully at the wickets, the posts, which were leaning at illegal and unplayable angles. I was standing next to Martin, searching for Lily, who I was sure was in that group of women smoking cigarettes under the last oak in Shady Oaks. I couldn't find her, but I did see Alexis Falvo.

I'd known Alexis since we moved to Shady Oaks a year earlier. We'd attended the same parties; she was the one who, at her and her husband Benji's Bastille Day party, had drawn a thin mustache on my face with a makeup pencil. I knew that she and Benji had had some marital problems back in Bristol, Rhode Island, something to do with not wanting kids or not being able to have them. She was kind and self-deprecating, I think I recognized that; she had happy brown eyes and a fine, lovely smirk and I remembered, from one party or another, that she had a nice way, in conversation, of making boring people less boring. She was beautiful, objectively, there was no arguing otherwise. I might have heard her laugh once, and her laugh might have been musical, might have been horsey. I was pretty sure she had once been a dancer, but then again she was thin and maybe she just looked like a dancer. Other than that, and like Amy Vincent, I'd never really noticed her. But I saw Alexis now, and she saw me, too; our eyes didn't move from each other. There was a promise implicit in all this looking; if Martin came to our houses one more time, which he would, then we would no longer try to ward off the unruly world, then we would do exactly what all the relevant sacred vows said we should not do. If that happened, then her Benji and my Lily and my sons would leave us. Our lives would be over, I was sure of this. Then why would we do such a thing? Why would we hurt the ones we loved? Because she was looking at me and I at her and we wanted, needed, to find out why two married people were looking at each other with such heat, and what would come from all this looking. This is not an excuse; this is not a reason good enough to be called a reason. The only thing I can say is there are so many ways you can destroy your life, but this one was going to be ours.

And then—and as I hear it now, this was a voice not of a particular neighbor, but rather all neighbors, the überneighbor, the great porch-sitting busybody and diligent lawn waterer who cares not about our inner craggy canyons but about smoothing our surfaces—someone yelled out, "Martin, I think your family's here." Martin walked through the house and out the door and we all followed him. There were his wife and daughters, standing at the end of the cul-de-sac in front of their new house. Martin broke into a run down the street; he hugged them all, one by one, then all together. His wife started crying these great heaving sobs. Martin made shushing sounds. "Everything is going to be fine," I heard him say. Then the family turned to enter their house—first the daughters, then Martin, and finally, his wife, who I know now to be Eliza. Before shutting the door, Eliza shot a quick look at the depraved, scary bunch we no doubt appeared to be, then closed the door and locked it behind her.

She locked the door! I could hear it, I'm sure all of us could hear the click and slide of the bolt into its hole. It was like hearing the hard truth for the first time. We could not stop ourselves from being ourselves, our pasts from being our pasts. But we could make a small concession. We could lock our doors at night. That could be mostly easily done. And that is what we did. Lily and I found each other and the party dispersed and we locked our door that night and got some sleep.

That was it. We lock our doors every night, now. Martin doesn't come visit us anymore. The boys are doing well in school. Eden wouldn't have been a patch on Lily's garden. Enrollment numbers are good at the university. Alexis and Benji Falvo's trips to the fertility clinic have paid off; they're having twins. Martin and his family hosted a lovely Canada Day party just last week. Things are back to normal. Everyone here is happy.

The Apology

Wyatt and Dave were in Wyatt's attached garage, searching for a croquet set Wyatt insisted he had bought once, long ago, that had to be in the garage *somewhere*, and while they were looking they got to talking, idly, about the weather, baseball, the status of their job searches, and the conversation took a surprising turn or two and soon Wyatt and Dave discovered that they had both been abused by Catholic priests when they were boys.

Once that was out in the open, Wyatt and Dave forgot all about croquet. From the mouth of the garage they could see their wives—Susan and Rachel—smoking Merits under the last remaining mature oak in Shady Oaks, which was the name of their subdivision. Wyatt's three sons were playing a complicated game involving a Frisbee, a dog, a detached piece of rusty gutter extension, and someone's hat. They all of a sudden seemed very far away, as if they were someone else's wives and children, as if Wyatt and Dave were very far from the selves they once were. Wyatt could smell the chemicals from the slow-burning charcoal fire he'd set earlier. As was the case with every barbecue he hosted, Wyatt had already made a big speech about cooking with charcoal and not propane. But now that he and Dave had ripped open their chests and revealed their tortured hearts, he felt very far from the man who had been so adamant about the superior taste of ground beef cooked over charcoal, too.

As for Dave, he felt something different. He and Rachel's baby son had died just two months earlier, of crib death. The doctor had told them that it happened more often than people think, but news of its surprising frequency did not make Dave or Rachel feel any better. The doctor had also asked them if they had put their son to sleep on his stomach or his back. "He liked to sleep on his side," Dave said. The doctor had nodded sadly, as if sleeping on one's side were the problem, which pretty much ruined what was left of Dave to ruin. Every night Dave had sneaked into his son's room to watch his son sleep on his side and in doing so he had begun to feel the blossoming of his own loving, fatherly self. Now that he and Wyatt had told the truth about their abuse, he could start thinking about that and stop thinking about his dead baby.

But he didn't say any of this. Instead, he said, "I don't want to be like one of those guys on TV." He was talking about the many other men who'd been sexually abused by Catholic priest in their youths, those legions of sad, wide-eyed men you see on TV who tell their stories in public for reasons—money? attention? forgiveness? peace of mind? the well-being of other potential victims?—that seemed mysterious, even to them. No, Dave didn't want to be those men, didn't want what they wanted.

"But what do we want?" Wyatt asked.

"We want an apology," Dave said.

He was right. They simply wanted an apology. So Dave and Wyatt abandoned the garage and set off for St. Anthony's.

Rachel and Susan were finishing their cigarettes when they noticed their husbands walking down the street, away from the garage and the smoldering charcoal briquettes and their chirping children and their smoking wives.

"Dave, where are you going?" Rachel asked.

"We're going to St. Anthony's."

"What for?"

"To demand an apology," he said, and kept on walking.

This was not the first time Dave and Wyatt had demanded an apology. Dave had demanded an apology from his bank for sandbagging him with hidden withdrawal fees. Wyatt had demanded an apology from his children's teachers for making assumptions about how much time Wyatt did or did not spend with his sons going over their homework. Dave and Wyatt had both demanded apologies from Lance Paper Co. for transferring them from jobs in Utica, New York, and Worcester, Massachusetts, respectively, to Clemson, South Carolina, without giving them a real say in the matter, and then they demanded an apology from their new bosses in South Carolina for laying them off not six months after they'd uprooted themselves and their families. When Dave and Wyatt were done demanding their apologies, they had apologized to their wives for not getting the apologies they felt they deserved, or for getting the apologies and then being disappointed that those apologies didn't make the sun any brighter and the grass any greener and their lives any happier.

So Dave and Wyatt had demanded other apologies. But this was the first time they had walked to demand one. It was a longer walk than they'd reckoned. For one thing, Dave and Wyatt never walked anywhere anymore, a fact their physicians couldn't say enough about vis-à-vis Dave's and Wyatt's hanging bellies and high blood pressure and diminishing life expectations, and every quarter mile or so Dave and Wyatt had to pretend to look at a bird or something so that they could stop and catch their breath. For another thing, Shady Oaks didn't have sidewalks. Plus, theirs was one of those pickup truck subdivisions and the S-10s roared by, going well above the posted thirty miles per hour limit and sending Dave and Wyatt diving into the street gutters their taxes had been raised for. Wyatt—whose belly was bigger than Dave's and whose blood pressure was higher—even raised the possibility of turning back and just driving to the church in their own S-10s, or maybe just making the trek some other time, when the sun wasn't so high and the heat so oppressive and the traffic so heavy, and when he and Dave were in better physical condition. But Wyatt's suggestion didn't have much conviction behind it and Dave knew it just nervousness talking. Because they knew they were doing what they had to do, and as

Dave pointed out, that they were walking instead of driving was a testimony to their seriousness of purpose. Besides, Dave said, there was something biblical and symbolic about their walking, and Wyatt agreed that he couldn't really imagine Moses driving around the desert for forty years in a detailed truck with running boards and cup holders.

They kept walking. It took Dave and Wyatt over an hour to get to St. Anthony's. In fact, they almost walked right past it, because neither of them were actual members of the church or had even attended mass there and they had only a vague idea of where it was located. Besides, it looked nothing like they churches they'd been abused in—nothing like Sacred Heart in Utica with its spire reaching five stories high and the cross at its peak extending another story; nothing like Our Lady of Assumption in Worcester, which was made of native granite and which took up a whole city block and was so grand and massive that it seemed like even God wouldn't be able to destroy it when the day finally came. No, St. Anthony's was more or less a brick ranch house, and they would have missed it entirely had Wyatt not said, "Hey, there was a crucifix over the front door of that brick rancher," and he and Dave turned around, gathered themselves, and then knocked on the church's front door.

Who knows why they didn't just go right in instead of knocking? Why is a vampire in the movies unable to enter a house unless he's been invited? Even a vampire wants to feel wanted. They knocked and knocked, and finally, a priest opened the door. He wasn't wearing a collar or even those black casual clothes priests wear: he was wearing jeans and flip-flops and the kind of collarless button-down shirt that makes you think of a rich person on vacation. But Dave and Wyatt knew he was a priest—because of course he had answered the church door, but mostly because he looked remarkably like the priests who had abused them: he had a full head of curly reddish brown hair and a cautious, fatigued smile and raised eyebrows and Dave and Wyatt both took a step back, because the priest looked much like both of their abusers, as though they had summoned those priests to appear before them in a single body.

"Can I help you?" the priest asked. His voice was tired, resigned, as if he knew the answer to the question before he even asked it.

"Yes," Dave said and explained how he and Wyatt had been abused by Catholic priests in their youth and now wanted an apology.

Dave and Wyatt really had been abused. Dave had been fellated on retreats, and the same priest had also more or less innocently and chummily draped his arm over Dave's shoulders during church school's discussion of the Virgin Birth and didn't remove the arm until the lesson was through. Wyatt had been fondled in empty church gyms after CYO basketball games, and the same priest, in front of Wyatt's parents, had simply remarked that Wyatt was a "good-looking boy." Dave and Wyatt had been forced to do some things that they couldn't talk about, even now, even with each other. They sometimes still woke up in the middle of the night yelling, "It hurts, it hurts," and had to be comforted by Rachel and Susan, who thought their husbands were merely having garden-variety nightmares.

Wyatt hadn't told Susan about his abuse, but he'd told his three previous wives. His first wife had wondered immediately if the abuse had turned Wyatt homosexual, or if it had happened because he had already been homosexual. Wyatt's second wife had used the abuse as a trump card, and if their checking account was empty when it came time to pay the mortgage, or if Wyatt accidentally spilled wine on the white lace tablecloth that had been in her family for centuries, she said, "Don't worry about it, Wyatt. It's nothing compared to what that son of a bitch priest did to you." Wyatt's third wife had been purely supportive when he first told her. She'd said, "It's better that you told me. It can't hurt you anymore. Life will be different now." But their marriage turned out to be something less than the happy, healthy thing she thought it would be, and whenever Wyatt drank too much at dinner parties and took long, loud stands that were somehow both offensive and boring, or whenever he failed to get the raise or promotion that he felt sure he would get, Wyatt would say, "I'm sorry, I don't know what happened, it's not really my fault," until finally, his third wife accused him of subconsciously using the priest's abuse as an excuse for all his subsequent failures and shortcomings. Wyatt hadn't told Susan, which seemed to him the first smart thing he had ever done.

Dave hadn't told Rachel, either, and didn't think he ever would, for exactly the reasons that Wyatt had had four wives to his one, and for exactly the same reason that he never, ever talked about his baby son's death, either. In the case of both his abuse and his son's death, Dave was afraid that once the truth was out there in the open it would be promptly lumped in with other unpleasant truths and its importance would be diminished; and he was also afraid that it wouldn't be lumped in with all these other truths, that it would dominate the others and that once it was visible no one, not even Dave, could ignore it if he wanted. Dave was afraid that he'd be accused of using his abuse and his son's death as an excuse, and that, at some level, there would be truth to the accusation.

So Dave told no one about the abuse and he never talked about his dead son, either, not even with Rachel. Instead they talked idly. They had so many conversations about the weather that Dave had begun to feel the same way about Rachel that he did about the television weatherwoman—sometimes she wore clothes that were understated and flattering, sometimes garish and unbecoming; sometimes he found her encyclopedic knowledge of tornadoes fascinating, sometimes dull. But he did not feel love for Rachel anymore, which before their son had died had been pretty much the only thing he'd felt for her. But at least he didn't talk to her about their dead son, at least she didn't make him admit to his terrible, true feelings—that the only thing that mattered anymore about their son was that he was dead; and not once did Dave tell her or anyone else about being abused, until he told Wyatt, and then the priest at St. Anthony's.

The priest listened, head down like a man in deep thought or deep regret, and when Dave and Wyatt were done he said, "I see," and then said, "It doesn't sound like either of you were abused in this church, though."

"Even so," Wyatt said, "we'd like an apology."

"Can you come back tomorrow?" the priest asked. "Or maybe the day after?"

"No," Dave said. "We've waited twenty-five years already. We want it now."

"Okay," the priest said. "But I'll have to talk to the bishop first. He'll have to talk the cardinal. Lawyers will have to be consulted. It might take a little while."

"That's fine," Dave told him. "We have plenty of time."

And it was true that Dave and Wyatt had plenty of time. They could have waited there all night and into the morning for their apology. Because even though the next day was Monday, Dave and Wyatt had no jobs to go to. They hadn't seriously looked for work since they'd been laid off six months earlier, even though they both had new houses and crushing mortgages and Wyatt had children who would eventually have to get their teeth straightened and go to college. Dave and Wyatt weren't old, either; they were still in their late thirties; they had the relevant college degrees; they could have gone out and found something: there were paper companies everywhere, and someone needed to work for them. But Dave and Wyatt didn't even bother looking. It was as though they had lost their will to do something about anything. It wasn't that they were lazy, exactly; it was that they felt that being ambitious wouldn't amount to much. Besides, Wyatt had the kind of oversized garage designed to accommodate the speedboat Wyatt talked about buying but knew he never would. Wyatt and Dave liked to set up folding chairs in the garage and leave the country music channel playing softly on the transistor radio and not talk and watch Wyatt's grass seed wash away in the warm, monsoonal spring rains. The rain made a nice, fat, bonging sound on the garage's tin roof; it was comfortable in the garage, safe. Why would they want to go out and look for work when they could stay in the garage?

Wyatt's and Dave's abuse at the hands of their priests might have had nothing to do with this lethargy. This was yet another thing they were afraid of: that they wouldn't know what was the product of abuse or what was simply part and parcel of being a normal thirty-eight-year-old American man disgruntled and living far away from his true home with no job, not even one he disliked. They would never know what was connected to the abuse and what was not. They would never be sure. This was another thing they would demand an apology for.

The priest made them wait in the church basement. Wyatt griped about this at first. The basement was carpeted and the carpet smelled of something wet and long dead and the glaring overhead fluorescent light kept flickering and if it were to go out Dave and Wyatt would be in complete darkness, because there were no windows and no other lights. Wyatt said, "After all we've been through, we deserve better than to be stuck in a church basement." Wyatt hadn't been in a church in ages, and he spoke longingly of the seed-oiled wood pews, the stained glass, the votive candles, the towering pipe organ, the holy water, the veined marble pulpit and stations of the cross. "I wouldn't mind waiting so much," Wyatt said, "if we could only wait in the church itself."

But Dave said, "No, it's better that we wait in the basement. It's better this way," and the subject was dropped.

They waited. They waited a very long time. They did not speak to each other. Wyatt breathed heavily through his nose, then began whistling in the distracted manner of a person unaccustomed to deep thought. Dave was crying softly, so softly that Wyatt couldn't hear it over the white noise of his nose breathing and whistling.

Dave was crying because he had started thinking about the apology—how satisfying it would be to finally get it after all these years and how maybe he could then forget about the priest, the retreats, everything, how maybe once the apology had been tendered he could start living his life—and then he realized that he had never asked anyone to apologize for his son's death. It had simply never occurred to him. He had demanded apologies from everyone and for everything imaginable, and yet he had not demanded one for his son. It was yet another way he had failed his son: he had failed to keep his son alive, and he had failed to demand an apology for his death. This was why he was crying; he cried for what seemed like hours, until the crying exhausted itself. You couldn't cry forever, Dave knew this from experience; and once you stopped crying, you had to do the only thing you were capable of doing. The only thing Dave was capable of doing was to wait for the priest's apology, and that apology would have to double for the apology he should have gotten for his son.

Just then Wyatt and Dave heard voices. The basement door opened; there was the sound of someone walking down the stairs. They both rose to their feet without realizing that they had risen to their feet. They expected it to be the priest, of course, apology in hand. But it was Rachel and Susan.

Wyatt was glad to see Susan, because he had begun to think his and Dave's mission was a big mistake: they had begun the quest for their apology together, on the same page, but they were not on that same page anymore. There was something about Dave's gloominess Wyatt could not penetrate. Wyatt knew about Dave's son, of course, and was so grateful that nothing bad had happened to any of his three boys, but he had not realized until now how much greater Dave's pain was than his. It had not occurred to Wyatt that all pain is not equal, and that one's pain didn't give one a greater insight into someone else's. Dave's and Wyatt's abuse had brought them together, but it could not do so completely, or forever, and so while Wyatt felt sorry for his friend, his best friend, he also felt alienated.

As for Dave, he was not thinking about Wyatt; he was thinking about Rachel, how beautiful she was with her hair swept back in the messy ponytail that would always make her look like a twenty-year-old girl just back from the beach, how she was much too lovely to be in this musty basement, how her beauty didn't make him feel any better and in fact made him even more sad because the beauty didn't matter to him anymore, and how he wanted her to leave immediately.

"What are you doing here?" Dave asked them.

"We're here to get both of you to come home," Susan said. "The kids are waiting in the van. We saved some hamburgers for you back home."

"Is the priest up there?" Dave asked.

"Yes," Rachel said.

"What's he doing?"

"He's just sitting in a pew, staring into space. When we asked him where you were, he put his face in his hands and said, 'Basement.'"

"He seemed a little freaked out," Susan said.

"Good," Dave said.

"Dave," Rachel said, "what are you *doing* here?"

Dave shot a look at Wyatt, who sighed his big man's sigh and nodded, and so Dave told the story. He spoke for himself and for Wyatt, looking at his feet the whole time. When he was done telling the story, he didn't look up.

"I'm sorry," Wyatt said to Susan. He knew his history, and could see the end of their marriage looming in the distance like a dark cloud.

Susan shrugged and said, "That's okay," because she was more than a decade younger than Wyatt, and her generation was relatively comfortable talking publicly about the bad things that had been done to them. "No big deal," she said. "I still love you."

"Do you know what I hate?" Rachel said to Dave.

"What?" Dave said. But she didn't answer him back until he lifted his head to look at her.

"I hate when I tell people that Nick died of crib death, and they ask, 'Where did it happen?'"

Dave smiled then, he really did. But when Rachel said, "I want you to come home," he shook his head and the smile disappeared and he said, "No, I'm going to wait for this apology."

"I miss him, too," she said. "And I'm truly sorry about what that priest did to you. But I want you to come home."

"I can't," he said.

"I wish you'd come home with me right now," she said, very

slowly, as if speaking to someone addled or retarded. "Because I don't think I'm coming back to get you." They looked at each other for a while, their gazes steady, unblinking. It was the way people stare at each other not when they're in love, but afterward, when they finally realize all the many horrible and beautiful things contained within that love. But Dave didn't move, and Rachel finally broke the eyelock and ran up the stairs, two at a time.

Wyatt was on his feet; he was already thinking how lucky he was to have this younger fourth wife and his spacious garage and his kids and suddenly the apology didn't seem so urgent anymore: he had waited so long, he could certainly wait a little longer. And even if Wyatt never got his apology, then maybe that was all right, too: it seemed to him that he had gotten what he wanted, somehow, without getting what he wanted, and he marveled to himself about how resilient the human animal is and thought that he might even work on his résumé when he got home, maybe check the employment ads in the morning.

"I'm going home, buddy," he said to Dave. "You should, too."

Dave shook his head. "It's all right," he said. "I'll catch up with you later."

They shook hands, then Wyatt took Susan's and they walked up the stairs, closing the door behind them.

When they were gone, Dave turned off the light and lay down on the rug. He was thinking of the future. His wife and friends were gone; it was undoubtedly too dark to walk home, and besides he didn't want to go there anyway. But maybe he could stay in the basement. It wasn't as nice as Wyatt's garage, but overall it didn't seem such a bad place to stay. There was an old Frigidaire humming in the corner. There was a bathroom with an exhaust fan. He could conceivably stay there forever. Maybe he would ask the priest if that were possible. Maybe he could attach it as a rider to the apology. Dave rolled over on his side in the fashion of his dead son, and his last thought before falling asleep was that he would waive his apology if God would just let him die in his sleep, just as God had let his son die in his sleep, just as God had let so many other things happen.

But Dave didn't die in his sleep; he woke up when he heard a door open at the top of the stairway. He got up and walked to the foot of the stairs. The priest was standing there, illuminated from above by the chandelier in the vestibule. The priest saw Dave, but he didn't move, and neither did Dave. It seemed possible that they would stand staring at each other forever; but that was fine with Dave. Because there was nothing left for him to do but wait for his apology, which was the only thing standing between the life he had lived up until now, and the life yet to come.

The Ghosts We Love

When I was eleven my father died in a tragic inner tube accident. If he hadn't, then maybe I would not have become what I am—namely, a forty-two-year-old brother betrayer, marriage wrecker, mother killer, second husband, ghost impersonator, amateur historian, and home renter. But I am these things, and that's because my father died in a tragic inner tube accident when I was eleven. It happened at my family's lake house in northern Connecticut, in August, during those last desperate days of summer when you try to do the things you've been doing all summer except more so. My younger brother Biggie and I were throwing inner tubes into the water, sprinting the length of the dock, and hurling ourselves headfirst through the tubes. And because this was one of those desperate last days of summer, Biggie and I were throwing the inner tubes out farther and sprinting faster and diving deeper and whooping louder. My parents were drinking their drinks—it was cocktail hour, or close to it—and watching us, and maybe my father was thinking the kind of deep thoughts I myself am consumed with these days—about time and where it goes and how easy it should be to get it back—because he got out of his Adirondack chair, drank down the rest of his gin and tonic, took off his shirt, walked to the dock, and said, "Let me see one of those." I gave him my inner tube. He walked with it to the end of the dock, threw it a little ways out into the water, took a couple steps back, shouted over his shoulder, "See you in the emergency room," then jogged forward and dove into the tube.

When my father came up, I thought at first we *would* be seeing him in the emergency room. Because he had dived too deep in too shallow water—the way he'd always taught us not to do—had hit his head on the rocky bottom, and now blood was streaming out of a big gash in his forehead, down his cheeks and chin and neck, down his chest, down all the way to the inner tube, which—as my father walked out of the water—I could see was too small for him and was stuck on his prosperous, middle-aged-man's gut. His face was dust gray and the blood was the only color on it. My mother rushed to help him onto the shore; she wanted him to sit down, but he refused. Instead he turned to me and my brother, the streams of blood carving up his face, and said, "And that, boys, is what happens when you dive too deep." We laughed, because it was just like my father to turn tragedy into pedagogy, and once, when our mutt Reggie was done in by a runaway Chevy Cavalier, my father turned it into a masterful lecture about speed limits and leash laws and why we needed to heed them. My father smiled, closed his eyes, as if satisfied by the lesson he'd just taught us, and then fell face first to the ground, dead, still wearing the inner tube, and so he bounced and rolled a little bit after he landed.

Like so many men of my generation, I've not become the scratch golfer my father was, nor have I joined the Kiwanis or the Elks as his father had done, but instead I've retreated to my study and become something of a history buff, well schooled in the past's whys and wheres, and hopeful that knowing what Lee did after his Lost Cause and Napoleon after his Waterloo might help me to know what to do after my own. And as any amateur historian knows, you must break up history into periods, stages, if you're ever to understand it.

My father's death was the end of the first stage, a stage where we lived in Worcester, Massachusetts, during the year and went to the lake house in the summer and thought nothing of family except that we were in one. The second stage began afterward—after the ambulance came and freed my father from the inner tube and the paramedics pronounced what we already knew to be pronounce-able and put him in that big, black bag with the zipper, after we buried him in Worcester's Paxton Cemetery three days later—when my mother sat Biggie and me down to explain how life would be from here on out.

"Your father is dead now," she told us.

This was obvious, and my brother—being the wiseacre he was and probably still is—began to snicker a little. I elbowed him quiet and said, "Yes ma'am," because I understood that my mother wasn't talking to us but to herself, and because she was talking to herself I found her scary, like those bums downtown near the bus station who muttered things about the world and the mess we'd made of it, things that made just enough sense and so you crossed the street so you wouldn't have to hear them.

"All we have left is each other," she told us. "You have to remember this. There is nothing more important in this world than this family."

"Are we going to sell the lake house?" I asked, because I'd been thinking about my father and his bloody, mangled head and the inner tube and how he keeled over onto it and died in it, how it seemed likely that the image would haunt me forever, but especially if I went back to the place where I saw it happen, and wouldn't it be better to find a house on some other lake, where there might be ghosts, true enough, but ghosts we'd never loved and so ghosts that could not hurt us?

"That house has been in this *family* for four generations," my mother said, sounding not like the gentle, wry school librarian I knew her to be, but like the iron ladies I now read about, those great women who stare down parliament, who rule from behind the throne and who throw overinflated pesos at the peasants from high on their presidential perch. "We will never sell the lake house," she said, and then, to clarify, she added, "Not ever."

That was the beginning of the second stage, the longest one, the one that lasted twenty-eight years, the one my history books always refer to as A Time of Peace. These are the stages that are dull and the most skimmable—because who really cares about Attila before he became the Hun, or Rome in between sackings?—and so I will skim here and say that soon enough my brother and I began to see the gene pool variations we were: Biggie became the black sheep who stole his share of booze from my mother's liquor cabinet and who dropped out of a state college or two on his way to becoming a high school English teacher; I became the A student with strong feelings about potential and how sinful it was to waste it. Biggie stayed close to home, in Lowell, while I moved to Dayton, Ohio, and became a VP in charge of packaging and shipping the necessaries Procter & Gamble make for us. Biggie and I both got married after college, but I had children and continued the family line—which, as history tells us, is mostly hubris and thus part of our downfall—and Biggie did not. Biggie barely remembered our father and when asked, admitted as much; but I thought of my old man often, in various ways—sometimes he was benevolent and peace loving, like the Jesus liberal Protestants worship with the help of their acoustic guitars; other times he was severe and totemic in his mangled head and his inner tube and much like the Catholic Christ, bleeding and suffering and full of holes on his cross. But in either form, my father reminded me of what my mother preached when he died: Whatever your differences, you are Chandlers and you must love each other. This is what Gandhi said to his Indians after independence, and unlike them, we did.

We did, and nowhere did we love each more than at the lake house, where we lived every summer. In the fall, winter, and spring we sometimes had our differences, but in the summer we were the lake house's weathered cedar shingles and the bending birch trees and the dinged-up, forest green Old Town canoe and the daily, leisurely laps we swam between the lopsided raft and the shore and the moderate, early-evening gin drinkers and good-natured, before-bed card players and the easy laughers and the baseball-on-the-radio listeners and the memory of the four generations of good Chandlers before us who had acted in the summer as we acted. The point is, we were better people in the summer at the lake house than we were the rest of the year, in the same way Idi Amin is said to have enjoyed a leisurely game of backgammon at his country villa, and Henry VIII was much more gentle with his many wives at his place in the Hebrides.

At the end of this twenty-eight-year Time of Peace my mother celebrated her eightieth birthday. This was in July, at the lake house. We were all gathered there—my wife, Elinor, our two boys and our baby daughter, Rachel; Biggie and his wife, Sarah—all of us sitting at the sturdy pitched-stained picnic table my father had made way back in our first stage. After her speech twenty-eight years earlier, my mother had never said much about my father or about us as a family. Maybe she knew she didn't need to. But that night my mother raised her wine glass, smiled at each of us in turn, and said, "I am the luckiest mother, mother-in-law, grandmother," and then, looking up at the blackening summer sky, she raised her glass even higher and said, "and especially, wife." We raised our glasses, too, and that was the end of our second stage, when nothing happened, when we Chandlers were happy, and loved each other very, very much.

This brings me to the third stage, the shortest one and the one I'm really here to tell you about. Like all important stages, it is not entirely clear where this one begins. Was Hitler not fully Hitler, the Nazis the Nazis, until he and they annexed Poland? Were the Mohawks done in by the smallpox my own pasty-faced English kin gave them, or, as some froth-mouthed Darwinist historian named Krebs claims, was there something inside them, some weak gene or rogue chromosome that was already killing them and they just didn't know it yet? Who can say for sure where one's third stage begins? Our third stage could have begun the September after my mother's eightieth birthday, when Rachel, my year-old daughter— improbable as it sounds and even though she'd never lifted any-thing heavier than herself—developed a hernia and died of it before anyone even knew she had one. Or it could have begun in January, when my mother had a ministroke. Or it could have begun in April, when Biggie brought a woman who was not his wife to the lake house over the Easter weekend, while Sarah was visiting her parents. After that weekend Biggie called me, said, "I did this thing," and then told me that he'd brought this woman to the lake house when no one else was there, had slept with her in the bed he'd slept in as a child and still slept in. Biggie and Sarah had been married for six years; they always seemed happy enough, and I didn't know what to say, but my brother had paused, as if waiting for me to say *something*, and so I asked, "What's her name?"

"Beth Ann," he said. "She's smart. Hot, too." This was the first time I'd heard Biggie refer to a woman as "hot," but before I could wonder about it, he went on and used all the metaphors in his vast English-teacher arsenal to explain how "hot" she actually was—what she said to him during, what she smelled like afterward—and I listened to the detail, closely, which was surprising, considering the modest Yankees I thought we both were. When Biggie was done, he again seemed to want me to say something, and again I couldn't think of anything and so again I asked him, "What's her name?"

"I already told you," he said. "It's Beth Ann." And then: "I really appreciate you listening to this, Nathan. I know you have problems of your own."

"That's true," I said.

"I think I might love her," Biggie said. "Please keep all this a secret."

"Okay," I said.

"I know I can trust you," Biggie said, and hung up.

I stood for a while in my kitchen, holding the phone away from me as if it might bite. My ears were full of white noise and my brother's lover's dirty talk and the buzzing of the unhung-up phone. The tile floor was shiny and operating-room clean and made my head hurt, so I turned off the track lighting and remained standing there in the after-dinner darkness. Toby and Bart were upstairs, playing some game that required them to make violent sounds—somewhere between a car crash and a hand grenade—

with their mouths. Elinor was at her community-center ornithology class, where she was learning the many important differences between those birds that warble and those that don't. That's who I was thinking about—Elinor, and the big trouble we were in. Rachel had died seven months earlier—the hernia had overnight strangled her bowels and small intestines and neighbor organs and the next morning we woke up and she was dead, she was dead—and I sometimes could still hear Elinor crying upstairs, gently and continuously, like a vacuum cleaner someone had forgotten to turn off, just as she had cried in September, October, and so on. I understood this, I did, missed Rachel and knew I always would. But Elinor had moved beyond grief into the unreasonable place we historians don't understand and are scared of, the Bermuda Triangle where some ships pass through and some disappear and we can never know why. I'd tried everything to draw her out, the way McNamara did with the Vietcong in their caves and tunnels. I told Elinor the boys needed her, missed her badly, and didn't she still love them, and she said, "I do love them, but it isn't enough." I mentioned that we should go to counseling, all of us, and she asked if there would be other people there, and I said probably, at least one other person, and she said that one other person was one too many, and no thank you. I told her that enough was enough, that it was time to move on, and she looked at me as if I were not her husband and true love but the sort of alien Hollywood makes for us—waving tentacles and extra slime and a single, centered, veiny eye Cyclops might be jealous of. And just the week before Biggie called I'd said in bed one night, "Everything is going to be all right," and she said, "You're lying. Don't you ever lie to me again."

I'm not a religious man, but later that night I got out of bed, walked to the bathroom, got down on my knees in front of the bathtub, and told my father, "I need help. I've already lost Rachel; I don't think I can stand losing Elinor, too. What do I do?" And my father said what he always said, which was: "Whatever your differences, you are Chandlers and you must love each other." And then he said, "The lake house, go to the lake house in the summer."

So that was it: we would go to the lake and try and get better and it would work. Because it had to.

Except now it wouldn't. Because it wasn't as though Biggie had committed adultery just anywhere: he had done so at the lake house, and by violating his marital vows where he did, he had violated the place, too. This was the way I was thinking. I stood in the kitchen and tried to picture the wind-whipped birches and white pines and the raft rocking gently in the sun-dappled water and the loons, the loons, and all I could think of was Biggie and Beth Ann and what they had done and where they had done it and how I had to keep their secret *and* fix my marriage, both, and I was pondering history's notable fratricides and whether I might add one to the list when Elinor walked in.

"Why is it so dark in here?" she asked. She was holding her Audubon guide over her heart like a Baptist would a Bible, the way two months before she'd held her ceramics textbook, the way two months before that she'd held an auto-repair-for-dummies manual; she'd taken so many classes at the community center in the months since Rachel had died that there was almost no hobby she wasn't expert in, nothing she couldn't fix or make with everyday household items. She gestured toward the phone with the bird guide and asked, "Were you about to call someone?"

"What?" I said, and then hung up the phone and turned on the lights. "No, no, I just got off the phone with Biggie, that's all."

"What's new with Biggie?" Elinor asked.

I know now that history turns on these questions and the answers we give them. What if the first slave trader in Dakar, when asked, "How much?" had said, "No, sorry, changed my mind, not for sale after all"? What if Oppenheimer, when Roosevelt asked him about the bomb and whether he could make it, had said, "A bomb? An *atom* bomb? Impossible. Can't be done. Absolutely ridiculous"? And what would have happened if I'd told Elinor what Biggie had told me? She and Sarah were friends, good ones, and so maybe Elinor would have said something angry and true about the hateful peckerwoods most men are. Maybe I would have agreed. Maybe we would have decided that Chandler or no Chandler, I couldn't kept the secret, Biggie was asking too much. Maybe we would have decided otherwise. Maybe we would have decided that just because my brother fucked another woman at the lake house didn't change the fact that he was still my brother and that lake water was still lake water, the house still the house, and it was still the same place we always went in the summer and were happy. Maybe I would have said once more that I missed Rachel so much, I did, but she was gone and I was here, the boys, too, and what were we going to do about it? Maybe if I'd answered Elinor's question honestly, things would have been different.

But I didn't answer Elinor's question honestly. I lied to her, just as she'd told me not to. Because family is family, I could hear my mother telling me so, could see my father in his inner tube telling me the same thing, and I couldn't betray my brother's trust. So I said, "Biggie and I were just talking about the summer and how great it will be."

"The summer," Elinor said, "great," and then started telling me why some birds have red breasts and some don't and I kept my brother's secret, and he kept calling, week in and out, telling me variations on the same secret—he'd spent more time with Beth Ann at the lake house; afternoons, mornings, whenever he could—and asking me to keep those secrets, too, and I kept them and kept them, until finally it was summer again and we were at the lake house with my mother and Biggie and Sarah, as always.

History tells us that most nicknames are an exercise in obvious-ness—they called Alexander the Great because he was; William was named the Conqueror because he did—but Biggie was called Biggie because he wasn't. My brother is a good five inches shorter than the six feet I am and my father was, and has always been at war with his diminutiveness. In high school he lifted weights twice a day. In college he wore motorcycle boots because of the three-inch heels. Even when he was a boy he walked around with his chest stuck out like a runtish rooster trying not to appear so runtish, which was why our father nicknamed him "Biggie," which is what we always called him instead of his real name, Phillip.

As we pulled up to the lake house that July—it was already near dinnertime and we were the last to get there—Biggie walked down the stone path to meet us. When I got out of our car, hugged him as brothers do after a long separation, and said, "It's good to see you, Biggie," he grimaced, shrugged, and said, "Yeah, you know, I kind of wish you wouldn't call me that anymore. Maybe you could call me Phillip. Or Phil. Either one."

"Sure," I said. "Phil. No problem." Although it was a problem, or at least I saw it as one. Because we all have those male neighbors with their midlife crises and their desperate divorces and younger second wives and their new, thirty-dollar salon haircuts and their sad self-deceptions and their elaborate attempts to pretend to be something they're not and these things never work out in the end and everyone knows it, and yet here was Biggie, saying he wasn't Biggie anymore. I felt sad for him.

But I didn't say any of this. I asked where our mother was, and Biggie rolled his eyes and said, "She's on the deck." And then, "She's gotten real mean, Nathan."

"I knew that," I said. After the ministroke she'd begun to send me letters—not her usual asking how the kids and Elinor were, but wild letters with no apparent theme except Disappointment and Loss. I'd gotten one just two weeks earlier, in fact, telling me how excellent my father had been with money and how she'd noticed lately that funds had been trickling out of her passbook savings and since I was in charge of the account (I wasn't, didn't even know one existed) that meant I was stealing from her—me, her son, and in the letter she told that sometimes she wished I wasn't.

"I repeat," Biggie said. "Mean. Drunk, too."

"She is?" I said, because my mother had never been drunk in her life. During our first and second stages she'd had one glass of white wine a night and that was it.

"Like I said, she's on the deck. Go see for yourself."

I did. Biggie helped us drag our bags inside, then went to help

Sarah finish unpacking, and Elinor, the boys, and myself went to find my mother. She was on the deck, holding a half-empty glass. There was an empty champagne bottle at her feet, and next to that a full one sticking out of an Igloo cooler.

"We're here!" I said, and my mother turned to me, and almost immediately I wished we weren't here. My mother's face had, as recently as the previous summer, seemed strong and youthful and her wrinkles had always spoken more of wisdom than age. But now all that was gone: her face was slack and mean, as mean as her recent letters. She slugged down the rest of her glass of champagne and held her right fist over her mouth, hedging against a belch that never came. Her stroke had affected her left side, so her left hand was in her lap, shriveled and gnarled up and useless, and her left eye and cheek were pinched into a skeptical squint, like a pirate.

"What I still don't understand," my mother said, "is how a little girl, *a one-year-old little girl*, gets a hernia."

It is said that when Bataygh the Tartar went syphilitic and paranoid and accused his lieutenants of plotting against him, his lieutenants pretended not to have heard him and began talking about the weather, how perfect it was for battle and slaying their enemies, and I would done something similar if Elinor hadn't first said, "Did you know that the state bird of Ohio is the bluebird?"

At that I looked away from my mother, and at Elinor. For months she could talk only through her birds and the facts she'd learned about them, but until now they'd never been used so obviously for deflection. I missed her so much—she was standing right in front of me, except she wasn't: she was somewhere out and elsewhere, beyond the lake and the roads leading to it, and since she wasn't there, I was remembering things about her and missing them, as if she were already dead and a ghost: the klutz she was and how she could trip and spill coffee on herself and look lovely doing it; the slightly antique words and phrases she used, like "rascal" and "for crying out loud"; the vodka she kept in the freezer, not because it affected the taste, but because she liked the way it frosted the bottle; they way she used to look at me from across the room, wide-eyed and happy, as if she had something to tell and no one in the world she'd rather tell it to. Now, Elinor was as far away from her former self as my mother was from hers.

"Now, Bob Hudgins," my mother said. "Bob Hudgins got his hernia from lifting one of his fat grandchildren."

"And the grackle," Elinor said. "Every seven years the grackle stays put for the winter. Sometimes he even goes further north. No one pretends to understand why."

"Terry Waldrep got his hernia from just sneezing."

"Pigeons molt everywhere except in one country," Elinor said. "They don't molt in the Netherlands. Or Holland, if you prefer."

"But neither of them was a little girl. And neither of them died, either," my mother said, her voice drifting off a little, and Elinor drifted off, too, back into the house. The boys went down to the lake to throw rocks at the fish. No one other than me had said hello to my mother, which seemed all right by her. She stared incredulously at the bottom of her empty glass, as if someone else had drank her drink when she wasn't paying attention, and without looking up, she said, "And you didn't save her, either. Your father would have saved her." With that, my mother pulled the second bottle of Brut out of the cooler and asked me to open it and pour her a glass, and I did, poured myself one, too.

Oh, how I would like to say that this was the beginning of the end, and that the end was brutal and swift. It would have been better that way, in the same way it would have been better for the Hundred Years' War not to have been.

But it wasn't the end. We rallied, as families mostly do. Inside, someone unwrapped the ground beef and pounded and cooked it into hamburgers; outside, I steered my mother away from the subject of hernias. I said how wonderful it was to be there, how beautiful the lake was, how lucky we were that the lake breeze was keeping away the mosquitoes and horseflies, how much we had missed everyone, how wonderful it was to be there. Biggie and Sarah emerged from the house with paper plates, plastic knives and forks, a red tablecloth for the picnic table. Elinor followed with the food—the hamburgers, plus the potato salad that always seemed to have been made that afternoon, every afternoon. We ate. The boys were well behaved, said please and no thank you and may we be excused when such things needed saying. Elinor sat next to me and our elbows touched now and then and she didn't visibly recoil when they did, and when a finch fluttered above, she didn't say whether it was a male or a female and how you could tell and why you would want to. Sarah told a funny story at Biggie's expense—about how he wasn't *Biggie* anymore but *Phil*—and Biggie laughed, good-naturedly, the way a man haunted by his cheating and lying on hallowed family grounds should not. I was really scrutinizing him, too, looking for signs of the philanderer, the secret sharer, the summer ruiner I now knew him to be: because we all recognize the villain from his black hat, his shifty eyes, his facial tics and maniacal cackle. But there was nothing: no sign Biggie had a secret or had shared it with me, no sign there was anything wrong with him at all. My mother kept drinking, but her meanness detoured into sentimentality and at the end of the dinner she said what she always said—how happy she was that it was summer and we were all together, again, as our father would have wanted it. We raised our glasses in agreement, and an hour later, we were in bed.

It should be said that we all slept in the same long room under the eaves, camp style, as we had done when we were boys and my father was alive. My mother, by virtue of her seniority, slept in the queen-sized bed, with one pillow for herself and one for you-know-who. The rest of us slept by ourselves in twin beds, and my sons in the bunk bed. It was as though we were all still children, even those of us who had them, but there had never been any problem with this arrangement. In fact, I never slept better than I did at the lake, in my own bed, with my family close by.

Until that night, that is, when I woke up to find my mother standing over me, peering into my face and saying, "Hal, Hal, Hal." Hal was my father's name. There is something more than spooky about finding your mother standing over your bed in the middle of the night chanting your dead father's name, and I've learned through my reading that Ivan the Terrible had the same problem with *his* mother. He moved *her* into a dacha next door, but I didn't have that option, so I did what I could: I closed my eyes with the idea that it, and she, would go away like the dream I hoped it all was. But it wasn't, and she didn't. I opened my eyes and she was still there, so I whispered, "Mom, what is it? Why are you saying Dad's name?"

She seemed not to hear me; her face was wide open and innocent and confused, as if she were a child and an adult had asked a question that she hadn't the life experience or the book learning to answer. "Hal," she said. "Where is your inner tube? Why aren't you wearing your inner tube? Why won't you talk to me, Hal?"

With that my mother straightened, turned, and went back to bed. I sat up to see if anyone had noticed this exchange, but everyone still seemed to be sleeping, and since I was the only one affected it didn't bother me much. In this I was like Ladybird, who didn't mind LBJ talking in his sleep about sending our soldiers to their doom as long as he didn't wake the rest of the family. After all, I sometimes talked to my father, too, often saw him where he wasn't, and there was nothing wrong with me, nothing that a good night's sleep couldn't cure, and so I went back to sleep and tried to get one.

The next morning was sunny, brilliant, the sort of day when it's easy to forget the image of your aged mother standing over your bed in the middle of the night, chanting your dead father's name. Elinor went on a long bird-watching walk in the morning, but it seemed to do her some good, and when she got back she was all smiles and even let me hold her hand as we watched the boys dive through inner tubes, as Biggie and I had done so many years earlier. My mother drank nothing stronger than coffee all morning, and didn't say a word about Rachel or the hernia she died of. She did, however, gripe about the big racket the boys made and about how Biggie and I needed to patch the holes in the gutters but hadn't yet and didn't really know how to fix them, either, and how our father would never have been so lax about home repair and discipline. I didn't know what she was talking about—my father had never been much of a handyman and couldn't even pick up a hammer without wounding himself with it. But I didn't correct my mother; instead I asked if she'd slept well the night before, if she'd had any dreams, and did they keep her up? She said, "Dreams? No dreams. Never slept better." Biggie and Sarah went for a canoe ride right before lunch, then came back praising the lake's beauty and how they already felt, only twelve hours into the summer, like entirely different people. I knew what they meant, too. Because isn't this why summer exists, so that the rest of the year doesn't?

After lunch, it clouded up and began to rain. My mother decided to take a nap, the boys wandered off somewhere to read their comic books, and Elinor and Sarah went to the grocery store. I went to get something from the car, and when I went back inside I found Biggie on the kitchen phone, whispering. When he saw me, Biggie's face got wide-eyed and panicky and he waved with manic glee. He was clearly talking to someone he shouldn't have been, and I had a pretty good idea who. I kept walking, through the kitchen, through the living room, and out onto the deck—which is covered enough by the white pines to keep you dry—to watch the rain blow across the lake. There is something hypnotic about rain falling on a lake and I tried to forget my brother and his illicit conversation and concentrate on the lake, the rain, the lake. But there was a leak in the gutter behind me. I could hear water dripping through, and all I could think about was what my mother had said—how my father would have known how to fix the gutter and would have done so already. While that wasn't true, I bet my father would have known what to do about Biggie and his secret, and just as I was thinking this, Biggie came up behind me and said, "Maybe I don't have tell you this. But I'm lucky to have a brother like you, a brother I can trust. I know that."

"That's okay," I said, because what can you do when your brother talks to you like that? Even Rob Roy, the fiercest of Scottish chieftains, was bound to accept the apologies of his most wayward and duplicitous clansmen. "Of course you can trust me," I said.

The rest of was the day was uneventful. We ate inside because of the rain, at the end of dinner we raised a toast to my father as usual, and went to bed soon after. I'd forgotten about the night before and was sound asleep when my mother got up out of bed, stood over me, woke me up by saying, "Hal, Hal, where is your inner tube? Why aren't you wearing your inner tube? Why won't you talk to me, Hal?" then went back to bed. I didn't say anything this time. I just lay there, wishing my father would appear to me, too. What about Mom? I wanted to ask him. Is she senile? Or is she really seeing you? What should I do about Biggie? Will Elinor ever come back to me? What if she doesn't? What about Rachel? Could I have saved her? Would *you* have saved her? Would you save me?

An hour later I was still awake, staring at the ceiling and wishing my father would talk to me, when I heard a woman say in a low, throaty voice, "I want you to take a picture of my pussy."

I sat straight up in bed. My palms were wet and my heart about beating out of my chest. I knew whose voice it was. It was Beth Ann's; Biggie had told me she'd said that exact thing to him the last night they'd spent at the lake, that she wanted him to take a picture of her pussy and keep it, so he'd remember it, and her, I guess. I knew I had imagined it, knew I was thinking about Beth Ann because I'd caught my brother talking to her on the phone, knew the voice was just in my head, but I had to be sure. I looked, first, at my mother: she was in bed, and I could hear the sleep in her ragged breathing. Elinor, too, was sleeping, her snoring light and adenoidal, the bird-watching book she'd been reading spread over her chest. Biggie's and Sarah's beds were at the far end of the room, and I couldn't see them, so I got up out of bed and crept closer until I could tell that they were sleeping, too, as were the boys in their bunks. It is said that Joan of Arc ignored God's voice in her head the first few times she heard it, which might explain how I managed to dismiss what I'd heard that night—although I wonder if, after hearing the voice, Joan managed to get any sleep, because I didn't.

The next day it rained again. My mother needed to do some banking in Worcester, twenty minutes away, and Sarah and Elinor offered to drive her. Toby and Bart had read all the comic books the day before, but they'd managed to find an old road atlas—we are a family who loves maps—and were comparing it to a more recent atlas to find out which federal and state highways had had their numbers changed. I was still bleary from the night before, so I went to get my third cup of coffee, but before I even reached the kitchen, I could hear Biggie on the phone. He was saying, "I love you, too, so much. I can't stop thinking about you." Just a minute before, Biggie had kissed Sarah good-bye, the way I wished Elinor would kiss me, and told her to hurry back. And how does this happen? How does it happen that the lying and cheating brother has two women to love and the honest, secret-keeping brother has lost his one? Is there only so much love in the world? If you lose someone you love, do you stop loving everyone else, too? These were my thoughts and I was about to have others when I heard Bart yelling, "Dad, Dad, come here." I came there, and found my sons jumping up and down, pointing at one of the road atlases. I asked what was so important and Bart said, "It's a pond, it's a pond."

"What is?"

"This lake," Bart said. "It's a pond."

Now, it's true that ours wasn't the biggest lake in Connecticut, or the deepest, but it was certainly a lake—Quinnepaug Lake, that's what we'd always called it, that's what everyone we knew called it, that's what my father had called it, that's what it was.

Except there it was, on the map, our small body of blue hard up against the red Massachusetts/Connecticut state line, and next to it the words *Quinnepaug Pond*.

"They probably made a mistake," I told them, and closed the atlas.

"It's a map," Toby said. "Maps don't make mistakes."

"Christopher Columbus had a map," I said, "and his map told him America was the West Indies."

"Christopher Columbus is dead," Toby said.

"I bet his mapmaker is dead, too," Bart said.

Biggie came into the room. His face was flushed and he was whistling a happy tune and he also looked taller, more erect, as though after all those years of pretending to be bigger he'd gotten what he wanted. He really did look more like a Phil than a Biggie, and I must have stared at him for too long because he asked, "What are you looking at?"

"The lake!" the boys said together. And then: "It's a pond!" They opened the atlas and showed Biggie, but he only shrugged and said, "Huh."

My sons are serious boys, devoted to the literal truth, and so Toby said, "We've been calling this a *lake*, when actually it's a *pond*."

"That's lying," Bart said. "When you say a *pond* is a *lake*, that's called lying."

"Huh," Biggie said. "It's stopped raining. I'm going down by the water," and then he left the house and went outside to stand by the thing we'd been lying about.

That night it was business as usual. My mother woke me up, said what she had to say to my father, and went back to bed. I stared at the ceiling, waiting for my father to appear, wanting to ask him more questions. Did you know the lake is a pond? Did you lie to us? Does it matter? Is it impossible to tell the truth? Should we even try? I hadn't forgotten about the lurid voice from the night before, but I wasn't entirely waiting for it, either, and so I was on the verge of unconsciousness when I heard the same throaty woman's voice saying, "You make me so wet. You've always made me so wet."

I sat up in bed again. I still knew, or thought, I was hearing things, but I considered the other possibilities. Maybe someone was talking in their sleep, but that seemed unlikely and besides, no one was saying anything else, now that I was wide awake and listening for it. It was true that the boys had been letting loose with the occasional "goddamn" and "shit," but we'd warned them against it, and besides, they'd never said anything remotely like what I'd just heard. So clearly I was hearing things. That had to be it. But like Geronimo and Crazy Horse and so many of our great, peyote-eating native warriors, I chose to think of the voices in my head as not hallucinations but signs, and in my case, a call to marital arms.

Elinor had never said these sorts of things to me, and I don't think I'd ever wanted her to. But we'd barely touched in the ten months since Rachel died. Perhaps this throaty voice was a sign, a sign telling me to say something, say anything. Perhaps it was telling me that things had to change, and now. Perhaps the voice was telling me, It's time, it's time.

The next morning the rain had passed and it was beautiful again. Toby and Bart were cannonballing each other off the raft; my mother was watching Biggie and Sarah swamp and clean the canoe, and telling them how my father had been a more efficient swamper. Elinor was looking at something in the trees through her birding binoculars. I'd gotten less than an hour of sleep the night before, and felt as though I wasn't entirely in my body—you know the feeling—as though I were watching another man sneak up behind my wife, put his arms around her stomach, and say, "I miss your pussy. I miss how wet I used to make you."

Elinor dropped the binoculars, lenses down, and I could hear one of them shatter against a rock. She made a little noise—a gasp or inward sob—as she turned to face me. There are so many things she could have said, so many things I wish she'd said. She could have said, "I know, I know, I miss it, too." Or: "Don't ever, ever say anything like that to me again." Or: "You and I made her, we made her, and now she's dead and I never want you to touch me again." Any of that would have been better than what she said to me, which was, "I'm pretty sure I just saw an Ecuadorian hummingbird."

"An Ecuadorian hummingbird," I said.

"They're very rare," she said, and picked up her broken binoculars, turned away from me and toward the trees, and I retreated, just as the Australians should have at Gallipoli, back to one of the chaise longues. I closed my eyes and tried to get some sleep. Because this was the lie I was telling myself—if I could just get some sleep, everything would be all right. But I couldn't. My mother was droning on about making a fire that night and how expert my father had been in making one and how no one would ever build a fire like he had and so why bother. But she was lying: I had a clear memory of my father struggling to make a fire, blaming his failure on the wet wood, the matches, the low quality of the newspaper, and so on before giving up and telling us to eat the marshmallows we'd wanted to roast over the fire unroasted, because they were better that way in any case. Biggie swam out to the raft, where the boys were, and I could hear him saying, "Do you hear that wind? That's a quite a west wind, isn't it?" I, too, could hear the howling west wind. Except it wasn't.

"That's not the wind," Toby said. "That's the highway. Listen, you can hear the trucks shifting gears."

And then there were Sarah and Elinor, standing to my right. Sarah was telling Elinor how good her job was—she, too, was an English teacher at Lowell Public—how happy she and Biggie were, and at that moment Elinor yelled out, "It *is* an Ecuadorian hummingbird, it is!" except I heard her yell it in the throaty voice I'd imagined for Beth Ann and it sounded lurid and it made me long for something and everything and Biggie was out on the raft, saying, "I'm pretty sure that's the wind," and Bart was insisting, "It's *not* the wind. It's the *highway*," and then I could feel the shadow of someone standing over me, and I heard my mother say, "You know, your father slept as soundly as I do. He never needed a nap," and without opening my eyes I sat up and yelled, "I'm trying to get some fucking sleep here. Will everyone just shut the hell up!"

I heard a collective gasp, but they shut up, and I tried again to fall asleep. But I couldn't, I couldn't. Because my sons were right: I could hear the highway loud and clear, as though I were on it, headed somewhere else, somewhere away from the lake or the pond or whatever it is we choose to call the place we think we know and love, but don't.

I didn't sleep that night or the night after, or the night after that, either. I stopped even bothering to try and fall asleep before my mother stood over me and invoked my father, which she always did. I then lay in bed, thinking about my father, waiting for the next voice to come, which it also did—one night saying, "Oh, you're so hard," the night after that saying, "Oh, I love it when you suck my tits like that," the night after that saying, "I want you to fuck my cunt," and so on. Each day, I'd catch Biggie on the phone with Beth Ann, overhear him saying, "I don't know what I'd do without you, I can't live without you," just minutes after saying something similar to Sarah. Each day, I'd try to say something to Elinor about our love and how I missed it and would we ever get it back, and she'd answer by describing whatever winged creature she'd seen just a moment earlier. Each day, my mother would give one of us, all of us, a lecture about what a great man my father had been and how we'd never see his kind again. Each day, I'd see my family through my heavy-lidded eyes, see them not as my family but as ghosts, ghosts I used to love, ghosts who lied about everything, even about being ghosts. Each day, I'd try to snap myself out of my daze by spending time with the boys, but I couldn't concentrate, and right in the middle of teaching them to overhand cast, as my father had taught me, I'd notice how puny the lake was, how I could see every inch of its shoreline, and say, "You're right. It really is just a pond." Toby and Bart would look at me balefully, as if they'd lost something, as if to say, "What are you thinking of? Why aren't you thinking of us? Aren't we enough?"

Which brings me to the end of the third stage and the night I'm here to tell you about. Everyone was in bed, asleep. It was around eleven, an hour to go before my mother woke up, etc. I had my pen flashlight and was reading a book about Communist China, and in particular about the Long March. Morale was low; comrades were dying left and right—from starvation and dysentery and the like—and those who hadn't died were despondent about how awfully long the march was and how it was never going to end and why not just give up. There was talk that maybe life would be better after all if they just gave up. So at night Mao would circulate among his starving, sleeping, bone-weary comrades and pretend to be one of the recently dead, a ghost who had nothing to lose and could do nothing but tell the truth. "Your family will be shamed if you give up now," Mao told them. "You are weak. You are cowards. You are lying to yourself if you think surrender will stop you from being what you are. Stop lying to yourself. I'm watching you."

There is nothing a true historian hates more than a reenactor, one of those men who lives in tract housing and on the weekends puts on the Union blue or the Confederate gray and drives out to some field and pretends it's Gettysburg or Manassas or Vicksburg. The true historian knows you can never relive the past without looking pathetic and silly trying to do so. But I am not a true historian, I am an amateur, and that night I was an amateur historian crazed with sleeplessness and haunted by a family that wasn't the one I'd loved and desperate about it. So I reenacted. I took off my shirt and shorts and put on my bathing suit. I crept down to the lake. I threw an inner tube into the water, dove through it. Like my father, I've developed a good-sized belly, and when I dove into the tube it stopped about halfway down the length of me. I wasn't brave enough to hit my head on the bottom, in the same way the reenactors aren't brave enough to use real bullets, real bayonets. So I went into the kitchen, sopping wet in my inner tube, found a bottle of ketchup in the refrigerator, dumped it on my head and hoped that, in the dark, it would look something like an actual head wound.

I crept back inside to where my family was sleeping. I first went to Sarah, leaned over her, and whispered her name. She opened her eyes and gasped, but before she could say anything I whispered, "Biggie is cheating on you. Her name is Beth Ann." Then I went to Biggie, stood over him until he woke up, and whispered, "You are my brother, you are Biggie. You will never be anything but a Biggie." I went over to Elinor, woke her, and whispered, "A bird is not a husband, not a daughter either. She's dead and never coming back. But I'm here. I am still here. Isn't that enough? Why isn't that enough?" I went to my sons, woke them, and whispered, "I love you, I love you both, but it isn't enough. You need to know this. Love will never be enough." And then, finally, I went over to where my mother was sleeping. I crawled into bed with her, on the side my father had slept way back in the first stage. I put my hand to her cheek, and she woke up. Her eyes sprung open, and she made a gurgling sound, a sound I know now was prelude to the heart attack that killed her. But I didn't know that then, and I whispered, "Maggie, it's just me, your husband, an ordinary man. Even with my inner tube I'm just an ordinary man. There is nothing special about me, or us. You are not even a Chandler, except by marriage; you're a Sant. There is nothing special about this place, this house, this body of water. I am dead. There is nothing special about that, either. Your whole life has been a lie. All of our lives have been nothing but lies!"

I am telling this now from a different house, on a different lake, in a different state. My second wife, Marta, is outside with her children and my children, all of whom are playing together in the water, making the cautiously happy noises children make when they are thrown together for reasons they don't entirely understand or like but make the best of anyway. It's been three years since my mother died, two-plus years since Biggie and Sarah and Elinor and I got divorced and Biggie moved in with Beth Ann (everything I know about Biggie is secondhand, since he refuses to talk to me). It's been two years since we sold our family's lake house in Connecticut. Marta and I have been married less than a year. She has had her first, second, and third stages, too, and our hope is that this, our fourth stage, will be our last. We rented this house, just like we will rent a different house on a different lake in a different state next summer, and a different house the year after that, and so on. It is a fine house, clean enough and unremarkable, and that is why we rent it, and that is why we will never buy a lake house of our own, even though we probably have enough money. There are a few history books on the shelves—biographies of great men and women that I've already read and will probably reread—but other than that there is no history here, and we like it that way. There is a guest book, too, and the previous renters have signed their names to the guest book, but other than that they have left nothing behind, and no doubt they have their own ghosts, but they are not our ghosts, they are not ghosts we loved, or ghosts who loved us, and so we cannot hurt them.

The Son's Point of View

The story begins at nine o'clock on a Saturday morning with one brother missing and the other brother lying backdown on the cool linoleum floor with his arms and legs out in the form of a perfect human X. The boys' father is outside the house, leaning against the family's 1973 Chevy Monte Carlo, smoking a Camel unfiltered cigarette. That father is me, but I wish I weren't the father in this particular story and besides, I am so much improved as a man and a father that I really bear no resemblance at all to that man leaning against that car, smoking a cigarette. So I will refer to myself in the third person as the father. I will call my ex-wife, Penny, the mother. I'll call the brother who is missing the baby, which is what we called him in those days, because he was only one year old and still in diapers and still young enough to be thought of as the baby. Nowadays, I call the boy on the floor Matthew because he is no longer a seven-year-old boy but a high school history teacher out in Portland, Oregon. I talk to him on the phone every six months or so and at the end of each phone call I am careful to say "I love you, *Matthew*," and Matthew is careful to say nothing at all. But back then we called him Matty, and so I'll call the boy on the floor Matty and I will try and tell the story from his point of view, which as everyone from my ex-wife to my court-ordered psychiatrist knows, is a point of view I rarely considered some twenty-odd years ago, when this story begins.

The baby is missing. Matty had been instructed by his parents to keep an eye on his younger brother, but instead he has spent most of the still-early morning lying backdown on the cool linoleum kitchen floor with his arms and legs out in the form of a perfect human X. His eyes are closed, too. It is interesting: you could easily lose track of a brother with your eyes closed—it was perfectly understandable how a boy could lose a brother in this way—but with the morning light pouring in the kitchen windows just so you could close your eyes and *still* see the membranous shadow of your mother enter the kitchen and walk over to where you're lying there lifeless on the kitchen floor and stand over you with her arms crossed over her chest and sigh dramatically through her nose and then set her jaw in such a way as to signify possibly huge trouble.

"What are you doing lying on the floor like that?" the mother asks, and then, before Matty can answer, she asks quickly, like it is one word: "Where'syourbrother?"

Matty opens his eyes, sits up, and says, "He's disappeared," by which he simply means that he hasn't seen his brother in some time. But his mother doesn't take the news in the manner in which it is intended. Her hands fly together in a tight white-knuckle shake and her face goes slack, which makes her look much older and much more haggard and much less beautiful than she was when, say, the father in the story first fell in love with her. Matty knows this because his father says this to the mother in Matty's presence, and often.

"What do you mean he's *disappeared*?" she asks. The mother is so frightened that she's angry, and Matty suddenly knows that he *will* be blamed for his brother's disappearance, eyes closed or not. Matty's brother, the baby, is his younger brother *and* his only brother and still a baby and their parents somehow operate under the assumption that Matty will naturally look after his younger brother and protect him and not let him drink any toxic cleaning solutions or stick his head in the gas oven or disappear without a trace. This doesn't seem like an unreasonable expectation from the parents' point of view, and Matty doesn't find it all that unreasonable, either, even though he keeps forgetting about it. "How long has he been gone for?" the mother asks.

Matty considers the question. He doesn't want to make his mother any more upset than she already is, but neither does he want to make up some fantastic story just to make her feel better. Making up fantastic stories is something Matty is good at and he does it with great regularity and proficiency. He could think of a couple big whoppers right now, without even trying. He could! The baby has gone down to the mall and signed up for a four-year stretch in the army. The baby is out finishing his paper route and he'll be back in fifteen minutes. The baby is out crawling a marathon and how long does a marathon take? Sure, Matty could say one of these things, but it seems possible to him that another one of these elaborate fabrications might upset his parents more than even a missing younger brother would, maybe.

"God knows," the boy finally says, and then resumes his position of lying perfectly still on the linoleum in the fashion of a man who has just slipped into a coma. On the floor next to him is a copy of his father's medical textbook. The textbook is open to a chapter devoted to comas, and what they look like, and what causes them, and what, if anything, you could do about them if you were a second-year medical student in a third-rate medical school like his father is.

One of the things Matty has learned from his father's textbook is that there are different types of comas, and some people close their eyes when they go comatose, and some leave theirs open. Matty leaves his open this time and so he can see clearly that his mother is already in full panic, but is trying not to show it. It's nine in the morning. The mother's hair is wet from her just-finished shower and she takes the time to try and put her black, dripping, seaweedy hair back in a ponytail. It is funny when you think of it like that: the idea of seaweed and ponies' tails brings weird images to Matty's mind of horses swimming in the ocean and getting tangled in beds of seaweed and then drowning, or of clumps of seaweed in the form of jockeys riding bareback on Budweiser Clydesdales. These are funny images and Matty laughs and then he sees that he shouldn't: his mother's hands are shaking now and her face— which has fine sharp cheekbones and sun lines fanning out from the corners of her eyes and which is normally pretty, except in the morning or in times of normal everyday stress—has gone so white that it is not even white anymore but rather the color of a lizard or a fish or some as-yet-undiscovered creature who has lived its entire life in a cave.

"Where is your father?" the mother asks as calmly as she can.

"He's outside smoking a cigarette," Matty says, because his father is nearly always outside smoking a cigarette.

With this the mother gives up on her ponytail and tears out of the house, her wet hair whipping her cheeks and neck as she opens the door and lets it slam behind her. Matty remains on the floor. What is he thinking? Is he thinking about his brother who might be missing, or his mother who is so upset about it? Is he thinking that he could have kept a better eye on his brother, as his parents have repeatedly asked him to do? Is he thinking that he doesn't know how he'll live with himself if something happens to his baby brother? Yes, he's thinking all these things, because he's that kind of big-hearted, sensitive boy. But Matty is also the kind of boy who, while thinking about these serious matters, is simultaneously entertaining the notion that he *has* slipped into a coma, because although he can see his mother facing his father with her arms crossed over her chest right outside the kitchen window, and although the kitchen window is open, and he can see his mother's lips moving, Matty can't hear her speak. Is deafness a part of being in a coma? The boy remembers reading that it is. Can it be that he's actually playacted himself into a coma? If so, Matty decides, that would be excellent. Matty reaches his left hand out to consult the medical manual on the matter, and then he hears his father say, through the open window, "God*damn*it," and the boy knows that he is not deaf and has not willed himself comatose and is disappointed.

I have said that I will try and tell this story from the perspective of Matty, a perspective I ignored for many years. Because, as you can tell already, Matty is a fine, smart, decent boy, a boy that any intelligent adult would be impressed by and interested in. Sure, he's a boy who lives in his head too much, a boy who could easily drive his parents crazy being so distracted by his own version of the world and not aware enough of the things actually going on around him; but he's just a young boy, after all, and what's so wrong with having a highly evolved sense of imagination? Yes, Matty is a good kid, a kid any parent would be proud to have as their son, and I want to tell this story from his perspective, in part, to try and figure out why I was not proud to have him as my son.

But I wonder if Matty's perspective has certain limitations that the father's does not. Of course, this kind of thinking is typical of the father, who as everyone knows is a terrible bullying egomaniac who doesn't give one damn about anyone but himself. But part of the way in which I am superior to the man I was is that I am willing and able to look clearly and honestly and objectively at all my former shortcomings, in a way, maybe, that Matty or anyone else I've hurt in the past cannot. For one, Matty, who's only seven and besides is consumed with his fake coma on the kitchen floor, couldn't know all the things contained in his father's *goddamnit*. He probably does know, however, that *goddamnit* is the father's standard response to the mother. The mother has just told the father that their baby is missing; but if she had said that she needed something from the store, or if she had asked the father if he wanted to take a walk, just the two of them, then the father would have also said *goddamnit*, because he was a miserable, sullen man who didn't deserve to be married to his wife, which is something she realized not long after this story took place. When she did realize it, the wife promptly divorced the father and moved to Portland, Oregon. But Matty doesn't know this yet.

Matty also probably doesn't know that the father's *goddamnit* referred, in a general sense, to the fact that the father was a second-year medical student in a third-rate medical school. Matty, of course, had heard his father call his medical school third rate many times, but what he didn't know was that the father never stopped thinking about the situation he was in, never stopped reminding himself that he was a failure for being in such a lousy medical school in the first place and that he was going to be a bigger failure soon because the father knew, at the time this story takes place, that he wasn't cut out for even a third-rate medical school and that he would flunk out before the end of his second year.

So, Matty probably didn't know these things about his father's *goddamnit*. Matty probably *did* know, however, that his father's *goddamnit* referred to the fact that he had gotten drunk the night before and that he was still horribly hungover. The father got drunk every Friday night. On Fridays the father would have some of his friends over from the medical school and they'd play euchre on the screened porch and drink bucket loads of Pabst. After drinking enough beer, the father was able to achieve a kind of amnesia about his overall failure in life, so much so that he allowed himself to complain bitterly about the medical school to his buddies. The father would talk about how backwardass the medical school was in its, say, treatment of severe high blood pressure and how they'd never do such a thing at pretty much any of the New York medical schools that had denied the father admission. The father was born and raised in New York, and his buddies were all from South Carolina, which was where the medical school was, but the father paid for the beer and so the buddies—who didn't really care all that much for the father in the first place and certainly didn't care for him bad-mouthing their home state, and who, as it turns out, were awful leeching hypocrites—were happy to let him have his say as long as he let them drink his beer.

Matty knew all or some of this because the father allowed him to sit on the porch, in the corner, while the father and his beer buddies drank and played cards. The father knew that Matty liked this, and the father also knew by his son's faraway look that the boy was able to sit there and pretend that his father and friends were not drunken, underachieving yahoos but rather were great geniuses discussing matters of utmost medical importance; he would listen to the rise and fall of their voices and the slamming of cards on the table and imagine long conversations in which his father, who was Jonas Salk, would take principled stands about medical ethics and patient rights and genetic experimentation and so on. Matty had an active enough imagination to sustain this illusion and was well behaved enough to sit there quietly in the corner every Friday and not say a word. The father would get drunk enough to feel proud of his son, sitting there so quietly in the corner, and in celebration he would drink even more and soon he would be drunk enough to totally forget that his son was even sitting there in the corner, imagining him to be the father he was not. This was what happened the night before the baby went missing: the father forgot all about Matty sitting in the corner and got extremely drunk and at one point yelled over the voices of his friends, "I'm telling you for the last time. I will never, ever watch fucking NASCAR," and then stood up to emphasize his point and in doing so tangled his legs on the chair legs somehow and fell backwards in his chair, breaking the chair and ending up backdown on the splintery wooden floor, not a foot away from where Matty was sitting there in the corner, staring at him in a way that told the father that the illusion of Jonas Salk had disintegrated and that the boy was left with his drunk father, who probably didn't even know who Jonas Salk was and who probably hadn't read the chapter about comas in his textbook, either. And so the father, who wasn't too drunk to be ashamed of himself, told Matty: "Get the hell to bed."

So this is another thing the father is thinking of when he says *goddamnit* upon hearing the news of his baby son's disappearance. He's thinking of how embarrassed he was in front of his son the night before, and he's also thinking of how embarrassing it will be to walk around the neighborhood, from house to house, asking his neighbors if they've seen his son, his other son, his baby boy, whom Matty, the older son, was supposed to keep an eye on but did not, and who has now disappeared.

Matty continues to lie there on the floor, watching his parents mouth things to each other on the other side of the kitchen window. He can't hear what they're saying, but he wants the words to be competent, reassuring, loving, and so they are. In Matty's mind his parents are saying things like: "Don't worry, he'll be fine, I promise," and "He's got to be around here *somewhere*," and "You are *not* a horrible mother, don't say that." Matty knows the opposite is probably true: that the mother is frantic, pessimistic, already on the verge of weeping about her lost baby, her dead baby, her maimed baby, and that the father is probably agreeing with his wife that she *is* a horrible mother, even if he doesn't really mean it, even if the father is too busy worrying about money and missing babies and *life* to be as pleasant as people want him to be. But as long as Matty can't hear these things, he can pretend otherwise, which, as everyone knows, he does very well.

Matty watches as his father finishes his cigarette, throws it to the ground, lights another one, and then stomps off down the street toward a neighbor's house. The father has big feet, a giant's feet, and the ground shakes when he walks. Perhaps this is what the mother is thinking, too, because she watches her husband stomp away, shakes her head, and then turns back to the house. She enters the house, walks past her son lying there on the floor, goes into the bedroom, comes out again, starts moving from room to room, yelling the baby's name, turning over cushions and mattresses and opening drawers and cabinets. Matty still doesn't move off the floor, but he's no longer comatose; he's through with that, because if he were still in a coma, a *real* coma, then he would not fully be able to appreciate the blur of his mother's ankles and feet and shins as they run in and out of the kitchen. It is a view available only, say, to a worm or a dust bunny. The boy considers, for a moment, whether to be a worm or a dust bunny, until the mother, on her way out the door, kneels down next to Matty and says, "I could use your help?"

It is a question more than an request: this is how the mother normally talks to Matty, because she sees the father order Matty around, and she knows how awful it makes Matty feel and so she tries to engage him, to treat him like the smart, decent kid he is. Matty knows this about his parents, knows the difference between his mother and father. Because in truth, he is more like his mother in every way and so obviously favors her, pays more attention to her than he does his father, treats her with more respect, even if she has that aggravating way of asking questions instead of just *saying* something. Yes, Matty actually *listens* to her, which is something the father wishes his son would do to him *just once*. Yes, for his mother, Matty exits his head, thinks carefully and realistically about the question a minute, and then says: "I'll hold down the fort. In case he comes back. Or someone brings him back."

"Thank you," the mother says, and then kisses her son on the forehead. Because she realizes that while her baby is missing, her other son needs her. She kisses Matty again, and then runs out of the house.

Matty gets up, follows his mother out the door, sits on the wooden steps, and watches as the mother and the father scour the neighborhood for his brother. They are going from house to house, they are yelling out his brother's name (the mother's voice as if coaxing a cat out of tree, the father's as if warning a dog to stay away from the garbage), they are knocking on neighbors' doors, asking, "Have you seen our son, our youngest son?" None of the neighbors have seen him. This goes on for about fifteen minutes, Matty watching his parents' grim, futile search from the side steps of the house. They knock on fifteen doors in fifteen minutes, and they haven't even moved beyond the immediate neighborhood yet. There are so many more houses, Matty thinks, so many more doors to knock on, so many more people to say, "No, I'm sorry, I haven't seen him." Matty sits there and knows that the world is huge, big enough for a baby to get lost in and never get found, and he shivers with the thought of his brother out there and at the mercy of the big, cruel world, shivers even though it is already ninety degrees out and the wind is like a weak spit of hot breath through the space in between your two front teeth.

After fifteen minutes, the mother returns to the house. Her eyes are pink, watery slits. She has the back of her hand against her forehead, a melodramatic gesture that undoubtedly she has learned from the TV, which is on so much that you can't blame Matty for being so flaky, the way he is, now and then.

"Has the baby come back?" the mother asks, and then, since Matty knows that she knows that the baby has not come back, says: "Do you have *any* idea where your brother might be?"

"He might be dead," Matty says. To be fair, Matty intends this odd, even outright creepy statement as a fact, not a hope or even a prediction, because he's still thinking of how huge the world is, how many doors there are in the world, how many people behind their doors you should be afraid of.

"*What?*"

"It doesn't look good," he says.

"Don't say that."

"I'm sorry," the boy says. "It's a parent's worst nightmare," which is something he also has heard on the TV, which goes to show that the mother does, in fact, keep the TV on too damn much and that it's going to rot Matty's brain if she isn't careful. Then Matty starts humming a funeral march, except he doesn't know any funeral march. He does know "Pomp and Circumstance" from his kindergarten graduation ceremony, so he hums that.

The mother doesn't even stop to question Matty any further; she turns and runs away from Matty, past the father, who is stomping up the street toward the house to get money to buy more cigarettes. The father sees the mother weeping hysterically as she runs by, and sees that she has come from the direction of Matty, who is sitting on the steps, watching his father process the sight of his weeping wife, watching his father put two and two together. The father stops for a second to follow the path of his weeping wife, then stomps double-time toward Matty, the huge world shrinking and shrinking until finally it is just the father standing there, hovering over his son. The father is like the sun, way up there hovering over his son, who way down there is the earth. This is what Matty is thinking, and he's also wishing his father would say something, wishes something would come out of the mouth that is as straight and cruel as a razor. But the father doesn't say anything: he just clenches his fists tight and bounces them against the sides of his legs. Matty is at eye level with the sides of his father's legs and the father keeps hitting his legs and hitting them and every time Matty hears the dull *thwack* of the fists against the legs he begins to think of himself less as the earth or even a seven-year-old boy and more as something that makes a *thwacking* sound when hit by a fist.

So there is the father, standing in an admittedly threatening way over Matty. I am still the father, of course, and I have promised to try and tell this story from Matty's point of view, and from Matty's point of view it certainly seems like the father is about to hit the son. I know this is so, because as I said earlier, I above anyone else can see my past mistakes clearly and I am a much better man because of it. And it's not just that I'm a better man than I was. "I'm an entirely *different* man," is what I tell Matty when we talk on the phone every six months or so and we go over and over this same incident and over and over the same minute detail every time we talk, because unlike me Matty is still living in the past and can't get over things that happened twenty years ago.

"Well, I can't just *forget* it," Matty says. "I thought you were going to *hit* me." Then, before I can say anything, he cites the relevant evidence against me, which is basically me hovering over him and beating my fist against my leg, which I did all the time when I was nervous anyway, and that garbage about me being the sun and him the earth, etc. When I try to explain myself, Matty just cuts me off and says, "I don't want to hear any of your shitty excuses, Dad," and then he hangs up.

A lesser man might cite Matty's lack of respect toward his father and his rude slamming down of the phone as proof that Matty is hysterical like his mother and not entirely reasonable or even in his right mind, for that matter. But I'm big enough to admit that Matty has a point: there is nothing more pathetic than a man like myself trying to make excuses about his past bad behavior, even if the badness of the behavior has been exaggerated to the nth degree. Because that's not the kind of guy I am anymore: no, now I'm the kind of guy who lives out his life quietly, modestly, the kind of guy who is comfortable in his own skin and who feels no need to make a big deal out of explaining away and defending all the bad things he did or that people thought he did.

Because if I were the kind of pathetic guy who felt the need to defend himself constantly, I would point out that while there *will* be some horrible violence in this story in the form of a serrated kitchen knife, and while it *might* seem that the father is highly sinister in the way he's standing over Matty with his fists clenched, he is not about to strike Matty, nor has he ever hit Matty, nor will he ever. And then, as part of my defense, I would try and put the father in some sort of context so that it would be easier to understand him a little better. Because wouldn't it be easier to empathize with the father if you knew that he is not so different from other men of his background and generation? After all, Matty, as well read as he is for a boy his age, can't know what it was like for the father to turn eighteen years old in a small mill town at the very bottom of the Adirondack Mountains in upstate New York and expect to work for the rest of his life at a paper mill just like his father. Except the father turns eighteen at a time when all the mills go belly-up or relocate to Mississippi or Mexico or wherever else there is cheap, nonunion labor, and so he ends up not having a job in the mills, and neither does *his* father, who gets laid off just three years short of retirement. Matty doesn't know what it's like to wake up in the morning and look out your window at Albany Street, the town's main drag, and see the line of red brick buildings completely abandoned, their windows boarded up and dripping with tattered weather stripping. And Matty, who has his own bedroom and lots of nice toys and books and plenty of space to let that big brain of his run wild all over the house, can't know what it is like to live in an old Victorian that was for years your family's own home until your father lost his job at the paper mill and was forced to move his family down to the first floor and divide the rest of the house into too many apartments with too many old welfare widowers and too many young women alone with too many children who made too much noise early in the morning and late at night. And for that matter, Matty can't know what it's like to feel the cold for nine months a year, especially when your family doesn't have enough money to heat the house properly and the tenants who weren't there five years ago are complaining about how cold their apartments are and how cheap your father the landlord is and the temperature keeps dropping and the snow keeps piling up, just like that anger you feel every time you stop to consider the dead mills and boarded-up business and the over-crowded homes and the snow and the temperature that is falling, always falling.

No, Matty wouldn't know what it's like to feel this much anger, this much desperation and violence piling up within him, and so he wouldn't know what it feels like to think you've found a solution to your problems, either. He wouldn't know what it's like to wake up one day and the snow is still falling, of course, and suddenly you just *know* that if you could just get somewhere warm then you would stop feeling the violence, that you would find the right job and the right girl and the violence would just melt away and you would be happy. Wouldn't it be useful, after all, to know such a thing about the father in this story? And isn't it relevant that the father, like many other men of his generation and circumstances, went south against the wishes of his family, and got a job working construction in the housing boom and went to school part-time and met the southern girl he wanted to meet, or thought he wanted to meet? And would it hurt Matty all that much to know that the girl the father met and married changed after he'd married her, that she was never satisfied, and that she convinced the father that he could do better than hammer nails for a living, that she nagged him into applying to med school? It was her fault then that the father wound up doing something he didn't want to do and was no good at; and it was her fault that they had children when they were too young; and for that matter, it was partly her fault that the violence the father felt up north came back, and it came back worse because he'd been a failure in two places now and not just in one.

So maybe it *would* help to know these things about the father who is standing over his son, fists clenched; and maybe it *wouldn't* be pathetic for the father to explain himself and where he came from, and would it be so wrong to have the father be seen the way he actually was, which is to say more human, less cartoonishly sinister?

But anyway, none of this stuff matters because I'm not the man I once was and feel no need to defend myself. Besides, I'm telling the story from Matty's perspective and obviously, neither Matty nor Matthew are interested in hearing the whole story anyway.

Matty sits there for a while, watching the father bounce his fists against his legs harmlessly, nervously maybe, but not menacingly at all, until the father says calmly, not at all meanly even though he has a deep voice so it just *sounds* mean to a sensitive seven-year-old boy like Matty: "What the hell did you say to your mother?"

Matty tells him. He tells the father how he said about his missing baby brother: "He might be dead," and then, "It doesn't look good," and then "It's a parent's worst nightmare," and then the humming of what was supposed to be the funeral march.

The father stares, dumbfounded, at Matty, and then asks again: "*What* did you say to your mother?"

Matty, for all his intelligence, doesn't quite get the father's incredulity. So he repeats what he's just said.

"Please don't be so strange," the father says. "Why are you so damn strange?" Then, without another word, the father flies out of the house again, in search of Matty's younger, not-strange brother.

And Matty is strange, and even though his mother—who is somewhere in the neighborhood weeping hysterically and over-reacting like she is prone to do—even though his mother tells him he's not strange at all, Matty knows deep in his heart of hearts that his father is right, that he's very weird, even if he cannot say exactly why it is so. He suspects it has something to do with the way he said about his brother: "He might be dead," and then, "It doesn't look good," and then "It's a parent's worst nightmare," and then the humming. But what was wrong with any of that? By saying his brother might be dead, Matty did not mean that he wished his brother were dead. In fact, Matty's saying "He might be dead," is akin to a father resenting the fact that he had kids too young and thinking that his life would be better off if he didn't have kids at all. But the father in this analogy doesn't wish those kids were actually *dead*, and Matty doesn't wish his baby brother was dead, either. Why would anyone wish such a thing? But, after all, was it not possible that the baby might be dead? Could his parents say for sure he wasn't? And did it look good, his parents running all over the neighborhood, ringing doorbells and screaming the name of his younger brother? Did it not look, in fact, real bad in almost every way? Were his parents not confirming, through their screaming, etc., that what was happening was indeed a parent's worst nightmare? And could one be blamed for wanting to hum a funeral march with all this death and foreboding in the air?

Of course, it was this kind of thinking that made Matty strange in the first place and aggravated his father so completely. And Matty wants to please his father, and wants to stop thinking strangely the way he does and make his father happy. "So just quit it," Matty says to himself and then strikes himself in the temple with the heel of his hand to make himself stop thinking and then smacks himself again and pretends to knock himself stupid—not into a coma, mind you, not even unconscious, just a pretend concussion—and falls down on the ground, right next to the steps that go from the ground up to the kitchen door, and that's when Matty finds his brother, the baby, sitting under the stairs, his sweaty blond hair matted to his head, staring at Matty with huge, happy blue eyes.

So now you know that the baby was not missing, really, and while he is not entirely out of the woods yet in this story, there is no sense in pretending for drama's sake that something terrible happens to him. Nothing does, no thanks to Matty or his mother or me either, I suppose, even though I've done more than my fair share of looking after him in the twenty-odd years since this story takes place. The baby is now a handsome twenty-two-year-old man named Steve who lives in my house and who works for me in the landscaping business I started once I flunked out of medical school. The fact that he works for me and lives with me and has for his whole life and we still get along says something about what a good, tolerant father I've become and maybe always was, the more I think about it. I don't harp on him for not going to college like his mother does on the phone from way the hell out there in Oregon; and when he gets drunk—which he does most every night of the week—and brings home girls in the middle of the night and does what any good-looking young man would do with them and then leaves them crying outside the front door, I don't say a word and am not judgmental one bit, unlike his mother, who says I'm turning Steve in a clone of myself. When I ask her to clarify, my ex-wife says that I'm turning Steve into a quote alcoholic sexual predator without an introspective bone in his body unquote, which is a hell of a thing for a mother to say about her own son. And while it's true that he's not the smartest guy in the world, not nearly as smart as his brother or his mother or me either, it's also true that Steve's a relatively happy kid who doesn't get on my case for every little thing I did or did not do twenty-odd years ago, either.

Because this is the theory I've arrived at since I've been looking at things from Matty's perspective: a son should never be more intelligent than his father, which is where Matty went so wrong and which is why I was never exactly proud to have him as a son. For instance, there was this time, about a year before this story takes place, when Matty was playing his first baseball game. Not that he was very good at it; he was real bad, and he couldn't throw or run or anything, but it was the kind of league where they play everyone. Matty was at bat and he swung at the first pitch and missed it completely. I was in the stands, like any good father would be, and I could tell that Matty closed his eyes when he swung, because the swing was so wild and because he missed the ball by three or four miles. So I yelled—and I wasn't angry, but it might have sounded that way because I had to practically scream so that Matty would hear me all the way at home plate where he was standing—I yelled, "Jesus, Matty, you got to keep your eyes open to hit the damn ball!"

Matty didn't keep his eyes open and he didn't hit the ball and he struck out on three pitches. I didn't think he'd even heard what I'd yelled to him until on the way home in the car he said: "You *have* to keep your eyes open."

"What's that?" I asked him, a little sharply maybe, because I thought he was criticizing my driving, which I'm sensitive about in the first place because of all my speeding tickets and DWIs, which Matty knew about and I figured he was pushing my buttons. Which, as it turns out, wasn't.

"You said at the game that I *got* to keep my eyes open to hit the baseball. You should have said: 'You *have* to keep your eyes open.'" And then he patted me on the shoulder and said: "I learned *that* one back in kindergarten," which I figured was a cut on my grades in med school, which weren't what you would call stellar and Matty knew *that*, too.

So you see what I'm saying about a son being smarter than you are: how can you be proud of a kid who talks to you like that? As a point of comparison, six years later, I yelled the same thing to Steve and he didn't correct my grammar. And he *hit* the ball.

Of course, if Matty would bother to look at things from my perspective, he might understand why he and I have the problems we do, and why I'm so much closer to Steve than I am to him, and why I sometimes consider Steve my real son and Matty someone else's. Because this is what Matty would see if he looked at things from my perspective: a son who corrects his father versus a son who doesn't; a son who can't keep track of his baby brother versus the baby brother who has the simple good sense to sit under the stairs where it is cool and wait for someone to find him.

Matty and the baby stare at each other for a few minutes. The baby looks like a miniature blond Buddha and is extraordinarily cute, everyone says so. Matty should be a little bit jealous of how cute his baby brother is, especially since Matty is a bit of a runt and pretty pasty and his mother has cut his hair in this ridiculous Roman centurion haircut. Any normal kid would be just a little bit jealous of a brother who is as cute as the baby, especially someone as homely as Matty. But Matty isn't jealous at all. He loves his brother, even if he doesn't love him enough to not lose him for going on two hours now.

Matty knows what he should do here: he should haul his baby brother out from under his steps and track down their parents and give them the peace of mind they so desperately need and deserve. But his baby brother looks so happy, sitting there under the steps in the dirt among the cigarette butts and lost pennies and God knows what else. Matty feels that it's an honor to be allowed to sit there and watch the baby and be let in on the secret of his brother's disappearance. But there's this one problem: if the baby brother decides to make a noise now and someone hears him, then the secret is out before Matty has even had a chance to be in on it.

So Matty picks up a penny from the ground, gives it to his brother, and says: "Is this enough to buy your silence?" The baby takes the penny, puts it in his mouth. Matty takes this to mean that they've reached an understanding. Matty gets down on his knees, crawls under the steps, sits Indian style next to his baby brother, and then promptly forgets about him. How can he forget his brother who was so horribly lost just a minute ago and who is now right next to Matty, sucking on a filthy penny? Because Matty is busy planning out the rest of his life and how it is to be lived underneath the wooden steps. This is what Matty is thinking: he'll have to develop a taste for bugs—for fire ants and palmetto bugs and brown recluse spiders—because there will be nothing much else to eat under the steps. And then Matty wonders, if he eats enough bugs, if he eats them every day, will he turn into a bug himself? On the one hand, it would be easier to live under the steps if he were a bug, because if he were a bug he wouldn't mind sitting around in the dirt so much with the other bugs. On the other hand, if he were a bug, would he still eat other bugs? And if his baby brother ate so many bugs that *he* turned into a bug, would Matty eat him? Did bugs have the same aversion to cannibalism that human beings did? If bugs did not have this same aversion, did this make them superior or inferior to human beings? It's an interesting question, to Matty at least, and undoubtedly he would spend the rest of the day thinking about it if right then he didn't notice that his baby brother is choking on the filthy penny Matty gave him just a minute earlier.

The baby is really choking: he sounds like a car with a dead battery that won't start and his face is blue and he's flapping his hands. Matty knows his baby brother is choking, but he doesn't run for help or slap his brother on the back or anything. He just sits there, frozen, as if he's watching a movie of someone else's brother choking to death, because that's what would have happened to the baby: he would have choked to death on that penny if his parents hadn't come back home, exhausted and frantic and at each other's throats about the baby being missing for almost two hours. Matty hears the parents coming up the walk because they are screaming at each other, but even then Matty doesn't shout Help! or I found him! or anything. He simply sits there with this shell-shocked look on his face and luckily for everyone the mother and father stop screaming at each other long enough to hear the baby choking down somewhere at their feet. Matty watches as the father's head appears in the crawl space under the steps, watches as the father sees what's happening, grabs the baby, slaps him once on the back, watches as the penny shoots out of the baby's mouth and the baby is saved. But still Matty doesn't move because he's still thinking about being a fucking *bug* or something, and only stops thinking about being a bug when the father—who has had enough, Matty can see this—grabs him by the arm, drags him out from under the steps, hauls him to his feet, and yells right in his face: "What are you thinking?"

I know I've said several times that I wanted to tell this story from Matty's point of view, etc., but at a certain point you have to say: Enough. Because if all we get from Matty's point of view are questions about the eating habits of *bugs*, who cares what he's thinking? So Matty's perspective is out. The baby is too young to have a point of view, so he's out, too. And the mother, well, she's so overcome with emotion at finding the baby, and she's so angry at the father because of some of the things the father said while out looking for the baby in the heat of the moment about her mothering skills, that her point of view can hardly be called reliable or objective. So she's out, too. So that leaves us with the father. And the father's perspective is: What a *day*. I need a beer.

So the father decides to go down to the minimart and get a case of Pabst. He doesn't tell anyone this, mind you. The father simply goes inside, gets his car keys, comes back out, and finds Matty sitting in the passenger seat, waiting for him.

"What are you doing?" the father asks.

"Sitting in the car," Matty says, and then, before the father can say anything else, Matty rubs his right arm, which is the arm the father dragged him out from under the steps by just a minute earlier. The father knows this is designed to make him feel bad, and he does feel bad, because that's the kind of father he is, even if he's also the kind of father who feels a little resentful at being manipulated the way the son is manipulating him right now. The point is, the father says, "O.K., you can come to the store with me," but he's also thinking, not saying out loud, just thinking: *Fuck you, you little shit*, like most fathers would think but not say under similar circumstances.

The drive to the store takes five minutes, and the father and Matty don't speak to each other, which you would think would ease the father's mood some, but it does not, because the son keeps rubbing his arm, sitting there silently, and the father feels like the son is *judging* him somehow. The silence puts the father in a worse mood, so bad that the father buys his case of beer and then drinks one of the beers immediately in the parking lot, before he even gets back in the car. But the beer doesn't help, and so the father, as he starts the car and heads for home, thinks about reaching into the back seat for another beer and in thinking about the beer misses the turn to his house, which means he'll have to go somewhat out of his way. Matty *immediately* notices that the father has missed the turn, of course, and of course he can't just shut up about it, of course he has to say: "Dad, where are you going?" as if the father has intentionally *chosen* a different, longer way to get home, and Matty is about to get all over his case about it.

This pretty much tears it, as far as the father is concerned. So he turns to Matty and says in his deepest, spookiest voice: "Matty, *I'm not your real father.*" Then, like your best movie villain, the father bugs his eyes out at Matty and cackles.

The father is kidding! Of course he's kidding, even though Matty is so strange and so difficult that the father sometimes thinks Matty is not his real son, sometimes fantasizes that Matty is not his real son. Even so, the father is obviously just kidding around. At worst, he's just trying to get a rise out of Matty; at worst, he's trying to rattle him a little.

But Matty is not rattled, or doesn't appear to be. He smiles a little nervously at the father, which is at least something, and then—get this—he *rubs his arm again.*

So the father feels like he has no choice but to continue the joke. He stops the car right in the middle of the street, gets out of the car, walks over to the passenger side, opens the door, and says: "Your real father told me to drop you off here. He'll pick you up in a few minutes." It just comes to the father, like that.

But does Matty finally get the joke and laugh? Or does he break down and start crying, like most normal kids would? No. He gets out of the car and stands there next to the father by the side of the road.

So again, the father feels he has no choice, because to say "I'm just kidding" now would mean he was backing down to his son, and as any good father knows, you must stand your ground with your children. So the father says, "O.K., then. Good luck," and then gets back in the car and drives home.

When he gets back home, the father tells his wife that Matty ran into a few of his friends and that he'll be home in time for dinner. Does he feel bad about what he's done? Of course he does, a little, but he also feels that he's taught his son a valuable lesson of some sort, and that the boy is smart enough to figure out the joke and also smart enough to walk home once he figures it out.

So the father relaxes a little—and he certainly deserves a little R & R at this point, considering the kind of day and *life* he's had—and by the time Matty finds his way home, the father has drunk six beers and is much calmer than he was and is feeling generous toward Matty and is genuinely happy to see him.

"Welcome home," the father says. "Dinner's about ready."

The son doesn't say anything, he's obviously a little put out, and if the father hadn't drunk six beers and if he weren't so relaxed, he might have noticed that the son looks a little crazy around the eyes. But the father doesn't notice. He follows the son into the kitchen, where the mother and the baby are waiting and dinner is on the table, and the father is feeling good, having his family around him like this, and still feels that way even when he sees Matty holding a serrated carving knife against his throat, because Matty has often played this game where he holds himself hostage and walks around the house with an imaginary knife held to his neck, saying: "Don't make a move," and so the father figures that this is just a more advanced version of the game.

It's not a game, but how is the father to know this? He's as surprised as anyone else when Matty drags the knife across his throat. First, there is the cut and then there are little drops of blood gathering and dancing at the rim of the cut and then the blood really starts to gush out of the wound and Matty starts to cry and gasp and shake a little bit, and his hands start to flutter like birds and Matty says to the father, "Dad, I've hurt myself. I'm so sorry. What do we do now?" and hands the knife to the father.

What is Matty thinking about what he's done? It is difficult to say: maybe he really wants to die; or maybe he's thinking that this will teach the father a lesson and if he survives, the family will be better off because of it. What are the mother and baby thinking? Also difficult to say: they, strangely, are looking at the father as if he's cut Matty's throat and not Matty himself. And what is the father thinking? He's thinking how unpredictable and scary and strange kids are, and that you have to be vigilant in protecting them, especially from themselves, and he makes a private pledge that from here on out he will keep his sons safe, no matter what, and that he will always look at things as they might, from their point of view.

Geronimo

Geronimo's scooter was dead and his real name was not Geronimo: it was Dale Lerner. Dale Lerner was a senior football player at Clemson University. "Geronimo" was Dale's nickname, but his teammates had not given it to him, nor had his coach. In fact, the coach had repeatedly refused to give Dale a nickname over the four-plus years of their association. The coach's logic eluded Dale, but as near as he could figure, the coach wouldn't let him have a nickname because Dale didn't play enough to *deserve* a nickname. This was a cruel piece of irony to Dale Lerner, who was convinced he didn't play enough only because the coach himself didn't allow Dale to do anything but run down the field on special teams once, maybe twice a game. When Dale ran down the field on special teams, he screamed like an Indian. Dale wasn't sure whether this screaming-like-an-Indian business was the reason for his lack of playing time or whether it was unrelated. He didn't care. Screaming-like-an-Indian was his thing, and he wasn't going to stop for anyone. On account of his signature behavior, Dale thought his nickname should be Geronimo. And so for the fall of his senior year he thought of himself privately as Geronimo, introduced himself as Geronimo, and people—teammates, teachers, regular students, graduate assistants, mascots—had laughed at his nickname and at how he had just gone ahead and *given* it to himself, which even Geronimo suspected he could not really do because of laws and etiquette and things. The nickname had not earned him invitations to team parties or earned him more playing time or caused even a single reporter to interview him. The whole experiment had turned out disastrously and Geronimo felt even more pathetic than he had when he was just a bench-warming senior with no nickname. Now it was the day before Geronimo's last game and he could not start his scooter.

It was a Japanese scooter, a Honda Aero. Geronimo had had it for five months. Geronimo told everyone that the booster club had given him the scooter, but they had not. The booster club had never given him anything. Geronimo had purchased the scooter from a blonde Kappa Alpha Theta sister for sixty dollars. The scooter was designed to bear the weight of the sorority sister, who weighed 100 pounds, not Geronimo, who weighed 280. When Geronimo rode the Aero, the scooter looked not like it would collapse but like it would be pulverized. If Geronimo were the mortar and the ground the pestle, then the Aero would soon be dust. The scooter was bright yellow, the color of a canary or close to it.

Geronimo had a theory on why the booster club had never given him a scooter or anything else. The booster club's name was IPTAY, which to Geronimo sounded faintly Indian. Perhaps, then, the booster club was offended by his screaming-like-an-Indian routine. You could never tell who you were going to offend these days. In retaliation for the booster club's thin skin, Geronimo named the scooter IPTAY and chanted the word every time he approached his scooter or parked it or thought about it. Geronimo had said IPTAY so often that he began to think of the scooter as more of a companion than a mode of transportation.

Earlier that morning, Geronimo's mother had called him, and they had had an argument about his future plans.

She had said, "Dale"—Geronimo had not told his mother about his nickname and she would not have used the nickname if she had been informed of it, which was why he had not told her—"Dale, you are graduating next month, am I right?"

"Yes'm."

"Let me hear your plans."

Geronimo had no plans, really. He had the vague notion that he would someday become a police officer and visit local schools and tell the kids not to do drugs and scare them straight if he had to, and then hand out signed, glossy pictures of himself frozen in a three-point stance, pictures that no one at the school had ever taken. He'd have to hire someone himself. Until Geronimo had that picture taken, he would have to keep his plans simple.

"IPTAY and me are moving home to be with you."

"No you are not," his mother said. She was a muscular, sun-burned woman who worked on the county road crew, and she did not see the need for nicknames much and did not understand scooters at all. She loved her son but Geronimo suspected she thought him dopey and a little dangerous. This was the way she had felt about Geronimo's father as well, and she had kicked him out and then let him come home several times too often before she had finally divorced him. Geronimo doubted his mother would make that mistake again.

"What's your problem, Momma?" Geronimo asked. "Is it IPTAY?"

"That's part of it."

"But I *need* him."

"It is not a *him*," Geronimo's mother said. "Not a she either. It is an *it*, and an *it* is less important than a he, she, or *they*."

Geronimo immediately felt like he was in a class—English probably.

"You gonna be an English teacher on me?"

"What?"

"You *conjugating* me or something?"

"Yes," his mother said.

This response made Geronimo uncomfortable in the extreme: getting *conjugated* by his mother sounded much more taboo then he had first thought it would. He decided to retreat to his original position.

"I'm going to graduate in December, and then we're coming home," Geronimo said.

"Grow up," his mother said, and then slammed down the phone. Once the phone had been slammed, Geronimo felt as if it had been slammed on *him*—on his toes or fingers or head. He felt like crying, which would have been bullshit, and besides, he was already late for class. So Geronimo went outside and tried to start his scooter. It would not start. Geronimo felt even closer to crying. He did a cursory check of the scooter's vital parts, which he knew nothing about, and then the gas gauge. The needle was on empty. Geronimo knew what this meant: he had forgotten to fill IPTAY with gas. Geronimo kicked the scooter and in doing so he actually *did* hurt his toe and actually *did* start shedding these little, sniffling, childish tears because his mother had hurt him and so had his scooter and now he had no other choice but to just *grow the fuck up*. What growing up entailed, he had no idea. And so Geronimo cried and did not try to even hide the tears. He just picked up his dead scooter and walked it to class. The walking cleared Geronimo's head some. It occurred to him that if someone were watching him— which nobody was—but if there were then they might have found the sight quite moving, this nearly three-hundred-pound man walking his scooter to class and crying and not afraid to show it. The thought made Geronimo feel somewhat better. There was no one watching him, but if there were, there was no telling what they might see. They might see a grown man walking his scooter with *dignity*. Conjugate *that*.

The class for which Geronimo was late was his senior seminar in modern European history. By some caprice of the university administration, history had become Geronimo's major. He didn't particularly like history, didn't know who had decided it would be his major, and didn't know why he didn't have a say in the matter. All Geronimo knew was that he had to get a C in this class if he was to graduate in December.

By the time Geronimo reached the building, parked the scooter, and entered the classroom, the class was more than half over.

"Mr. Lerner, you are late," the history professor said as Geronimo sat in his seat. The professor—Geronimo could never remember his name—had been lecturing on post-Stalin Russia.

"Mr. Lerner," the professor repeated.

"Geronimo."

"Of course," the professor said. "Mr. *Geronimo*."

Geronimo and the professor went through this same routine at least once a week. The professor seemed to take great pleasure in being corrected, too much pleasure, so Geronimo thought, to ever respect Geronimo enough to give him the C he needed to graduate.

"*Mr.* Geronimo," the professor said. "Why are you so late?"

Geronimo told him.

"A scooter?" the professor said. "You have a scooter?"

"The booster club gave it to me."

"We're talking about the same thing, are we not?" the professor asked, scratching the very top of his curly head of hair. He was a slight, well-dressed man who squinted constantly. The professor did not wear glasses to class, but Geronimo suspected he was the kind of vain man who probably only wore them at home, while he was pouring over his manuscripts or lecturing his wife about how awfully good Gulag caviar was. "A scooter is a very small motor-cycle. Is that your definition as well?"

Geronimo said that it was.

"Is it right outside?"

"You know it."

The professor said that he did *not* know it until this very moment. He also said that there were certain things more important than Khrushchev, Gorbachev, etc., and that the class would now drop everything and take a small field trip to see Geronimo's scooter parked out in front of the building.

The class did not move for a second, to see if the professor was kidding. He was not kidding. The professor walked right out of the classroom. Geronimo, who didn't want to be in the classroom in the first place, was happy to follow.

"You heard the man," Geronimo said to the class. It was the first time he had ever spoken to any of them, as a group or individually. It was also the closest he'd ever come to being in a press conference. It felt good, these eyes on him, and Geronimo did not want the feeling ruined. And so before he had to face his classmates' lack of response, he walked out of the classroom. The rest of the seminar followed.

Four floors down, they found their professor considering the spectacle of Geronimo's bright yellow scooter.

"*Mr.* Geronimo," the professor said, slowly, formally, in a way that seemed very European to Geronimo, and which infuriated him, "*Mr.* Geronimo, your scooter is bright yellow."

"Canary," Geronimo said.

"You are exactly right," the professor said. "Canary. It is the color of a canary."

This remark drew a small, nervous laugh from the rest of the class, but the professor ignored the laughter. The fact that the scooter was *canary* and that Geronimo said so seemed to decide something for the professor. He smiled very thinly at Geronimo and patted him on the back.

"*Mr.* Geronimo," he said, "you do not strike me as a man who is about to graduate from this university."

That said, the professor turned his back to Geronimo and walked away from him and the rest of the class, his leather satchel swinging and bouncing against his bony little hip.

Despite the fact that class was over, which was good news, Geronimo did not like the professor's ambiguous send-off one bit. Did the professor mean that he wasn't going to allow Geronimo to graduate, or that he couldn't believe Geronimo actually was graduating *already*? Was this merely the professor's egghead way of saying: *Time flies?* Geronimo couldn't be sure. He turned to consult his fourteen fellow seniors, who were gathered around his beat-up canary scooter like it was a dead dog that they had just found in the road and didn't know what to do with.

Geronimo surveyed the faces of his classmates. He knew none of them, even though they were all seniors and had been in many of the same classes he had. He didn't even know their names. There *was* this short blond guy standing next to him who always wore cheap plastic flip-flops to class, even in the winter. Geronimo remembered something about this guy's name being Phil, and that he was from Connecticut. Connecticut, Geronimo knew, was one of the smaller states.

"Phil," Geronimo said to the blond guy.

"Yes?"

"Nothing." Now that Geronimo had gotten Phil's name right, he had reached the far edge of their relationship.

"Did the booster club really give you this thing?" Phil said, pointing at the scooter.

"IPTAY!" Geronimo said happily. The boundaries of his and Phil's relationship seemed to stretch a little.

Like the canary comment, this happy outburst of IPTAY seemed to be a definitive moment in the minds of Geronimo's classmates. A couple of them gave him distracted half smiles. They cast one final look at his pulverized scooter. A girl giggled and then put her hand over her mouth. Then all fourteen of his classmates simply turned their backs on Geronimo and walked away. Geronimo watched them, strolling in small groups of two and three toward the library or their dorms or the campus bar.

"IPTAY," Geronimo said sadly, softly, as he put his hands on his scooter and began walking to the gas station. Geronimo felt the world was collapsing around him. But was this possible? Could the world actually collapse? And could you arrest the collapsing once it had started? His father, before his mother kicked him out for good, had once stopped their cellar from collapsing by using large floor jacks to brace the ceiling. It had worked, for about two months. Geronimo thought two months sounded pretty damn good. "I'd take two months," Geronimo said out loud. But a cellar was not the world, and if the world *could* collapse then it *would*, and there was nothing you could do about it. No, there was not.

Geronimo put gas in his scooter and drove over to a team meeting, which was convening on the main floor of the student union. The coach met each year with his graduating seniors so that he could impart some wisdom that would do them some good off the football field.

"Fellows," the coach said, "if a man cannot be moved by the sight of young Christian women eating soft ice cream, then a man cannot be moved."

Coach was referring to the dozens of women swirling and pacing around the student union, licking soft ice cream cones.

"Men," the coach said. "It is some wonderful twist of fate that the offices of the Fellowship of Young Christian Women were placed next to the Polar Freeze Tastee Stand. And it is some even more wonderful twist of fate that Young Christian Women take an extraordinarily great pleasure in some soft ice cream after their weekly meeting. But it is plain miraculous that today, November 23, the day I set out to teach you something about the way the world works, that it should be so ungodly hot, and that soft ice cream should be so desperately needed. Men, you have had a perfectly awful season and frankly, I'm ashamed of you. But at least you have this."

With that, the coach grabbed each of his graduating seniors in a tight, back-pounding hug, and then walked away.

Geronimo knew there was something wrong with his coach, who was a short, perverted bald man who looked more like a doorknob than a human being, and who, after all, refused to play Geronimo more than twice a game even though the team had gone winless that season. This was clearly a sign of the coach's dementia. But Geronimo had to admit that there was something mysterious and wonderful about these young, straw-thin women with crucifixes dangling just above the scoop necks of their tank tops, walking two by two, licking their soft ice cream very quickly so that the ice cream would not melt and trying to talk to each other at the same time and thereby almost losing some of the ice cream, which forced them into taking this gulping emergency action with their mouths. In their attempt to save their ice cream, the women often put their hands underneath the cones, and whatever they caught they would lick off their fingers, off their palms, the back of their hands, whatever bodily surface on which the ice cream happened to drip.

Geronimo found all this licking so beautiful, so *artful*, that he did something he rarely ever did: he spoke to one of his black teammates.

"You see that?" Geronimo said to the guy standing next to him, a black strong safety nicknamed Cheetah.

"What?"

Geronimo then pointed at one girl wearing a white tank top. The girl, incredibly enough, seemed to have her whole hand inside her mouth.

"I see a white girl with her fist in her mouth," Cheetah said back.

"Yeah!"

"A white girl sucking on her *fist*," Cheetah said. "What'm I supposed to learn from *that*?"

Cheetah then stared at Geronimo, as if he had an answer to the question. Geronimo did not.

"Yeah!" he said again.

Cheetah turned away from Geronimo, back to his black teammates, with whom he conferenced in whispers. The black seniors, about fifteen total, looked in the direction their coach had departed. When it appeared certain that the coach would not return, the black players simply walked away.

After the black players' departure, Geronimo joined the white players, who were for the most part still standing there. Unlike the black players, the white players appeared very content in their ogling of the Young Christian Women. Geronimo punched a boulder-shaped backup center nicknamed Herkie on the shoulder. The punch startled Herkie out of his ogling.

"What do you want?"

"What do you think of that?" Geronimo said, this time gesturing at a redheaded girl with a green ribbed sweater tank top who was slowly, deliberately licking each individual finger.

"I think," Herkie said, "that she likes you, Lerner."

Geronimo cringed at the use of his proper name, but he decided to let it pass in pursuit of the truth. The truth, Geronimo knew, was that the girl did not like him. The girl didn't even notice him standing there. Geronimo knew that the redheaded Christian girl was more in love with her ice cream than with him.

"She's not in love with me," Geronimo said. "She's in love with her ice cream."

"What?"

"She's a *Christian*."

"What are you talking about, Lerner?"

Geronimo explained to Herkie that, as a Christian, the girl was not allowed to desire a man to whom she was not married, but she was allowed to love someone or -thing *non*sexually. This is where the ice cream came into play. Geronimo told Herkie that if the woman were allowed to love someone sexually, then of course he would be a prime candidate.

This struck Geronimo as a beautiful, profound piece of rationalization. He was surprised it had come out of his mouth, his brain. He just stood there and admired the rationalization as if it were an expensive car, a Ferrari perhaps, or a Mustang, a kind of car to which Geronimo had always been partial.

"Bullshit," Herkie finally said. "She wants you."

Immediately, the profundity of Geronimo's rationalization disappeared, and he was forced to admit two things: Herkie was lying and yet Geronimo wanted Herkie to be telling the truth.

So he allowed himself to believe that Herkie was telling the truth.

"Are you sure?"

"Absofuckinglutely," Herkie said. He pointed back to the redheaded woman, who had finished licking her fingers and was back working on the cone proper. "You go talk to her before she leaves."

"I can't do it."

"Are you not in your last month in college?" Herkie asked. "Do you actually have anything to lose?"

Geronimo admitted that he did not having anything to lose. "But what should I say?" he asked.

"Speak directly," Herkie told him.

This seemed like useful advice. Geronimo walked up to the girl, who was considering the sight of this 280-pound man advancing upon her, his size 14 shoes pounding and flapping on the student union's brick floor.

"Yes?" she said.

"I was wondering," Geronimo said, "if you would lick me the way you lick that ice cream cone." This was not something he normally would say, but after all, he was speaking directly. Geronimo looked back to Herkie, who gave him a sly, waist-level thumbs-up.

The girl asked him to repeat the question.

"Would you lick me like ice cream?"

"Yes."

This was so surprising that Geronimo bent over slightly and made an involuntary caveman-like sound, something approximating an *oof*! Geronimo looked around to get Herkie's reaction, but he had disappeared into the pack of his hulking teammates, who were leering at the last stragglers among the ice cream lickers.

"Listen," the girl said after Geronimo made another involuntary *oof* when he saw that Herkie was not around to give him any further encouragement. "I'm almost done with this." The girl held up her ice cream cone: there was no ice cream visible, only the cone itself left. The girl took a loud, teeth-grinding *chomp* out of it.

"Yes," Geronimo said, barely getting the word out of his throat, past his dry, chalky lips.

"Well, do you want to go somewhere?" the girl said, finishing the cone with one last snapping bite. "I've got beer back at my apartment."

Geronimo nearly made the *oof* sound again, but reined himself in. He was not sure what kind of Christian girl he had on his hands here, but Geronimo knew enough not to further jeopardize this good thing with more involuntary caveman-like sounds. After all, here he was, about to get laid by a Christian girl with beer and all he had had to do to secure such a thing was to speak directly. Such a man did not do things involuntarily.

"I go with you willingly," Geronimo said. "We'll take my scooter."

"It's not good beer," the girl said, grabbing his hand. "But it's got alcohol in it."

The beer did have alcohol in it, and Geronimo, who did not drink much by virtue of certain team rules, drank two beers quickly and felt drunk. Drunk, he felt compelled to say something romantic to the girl, who was sitting on her couch next to him, drinking her third beer, looking a little bored.

"Your shirt, sweater, *whatever*, looks like a potato chip," Geronimo finally said, finding his romantic sentiment in the ridges and grooves of the girl's sweater tank top. When he got no response from the girl, he elaborated. "I'm talking about the good kind. The ones with deep ridges."

"What are you saying?"

"Your shirt," Geronimo said as he reached over and stroked the material. "It's interesting."

"Fuck all," the girl said, sticking her beer in between the couch seat cushions and taking off her shirt and throwing it in the corner of the room. The girl had on a peach-colored bra and her skin was peach-colored as well. Geronimo noticed that she even had a little barely visible peach fuzz of hair on her forearms.

"You look like a peach," Geronimo said.

The girl looked down at herself.

"Christ almighty," she said, and then unsnapped her bra and threw it in the corner next to her shirt.

"How about that?" the girl asked him, her hands resting on her stomach, which was absurdly flat, more like a back than a stomach. "Am I done looking like food?"

The girl, topless, looked more like food—like a pair of peaches balancing on top of a graham cracker—than before, but Geronimo did not say so. He just sat there, feeling a little breathless and tight in the chest, looking at this bare-breasted girl who was staring at him. She seemed to expect something, some sort of action. So Geronimo took off his shirt and threw it in the corner, and immediately felt very stupid for doing so. He crossed his arms over his chest, the way he had seen girls do when they were cold. The girl sitting next to him did not cover her chest. She just kept staring.

"My name is Geronimo," he finally said.

"Laura Ann," the girl said.

"Laura Ann, what exactly are we doing here?" Geronimo asked.

The question triggered something in Laura Ann. She stopped staring and scooted over on the couch, sat in Geronimo's lap, and began kissing him, first on the mouth and then on the chest and then she began licking him *like he was ice cream*, as promised. All Geronimo could think was that this was exactly why he had never taken steroids. Many of his teammates took steroids and all the starting defensive and offensive linemen did. Geronimo suspected that he would have played more in his four years if he'd taken steroids himself. But he had learned from the literature the coaching staff handed out at the beginning of each season that *doping*— this is what the literature called it—led to certain *erectile difficulties*. Geronimo didn't like the sound of that at all. Nor did he like the sight of the pimpled topography of his teammates' backs, which Geronimo also knew to be a direct product of *doping*. And now here he was with his shirt off and no back acne to speak of and no erectile difficulties whatsoever and Laura Ann licking him like ice cream *wished* it would be licked.

For the first time, perhaps ever, Geronimo felt lucky.

It was, of course, only a momentary feeling. In the next moment, Geronimo wished he *had* erectile difficulties, for Laura Ann, while treating him like ice cream, brushed the back of her hand up against his crotch. This was the unexpected final straw for Geronimo. He came. Laura Ann knew it. She looked up at him wide-eyed and scooted back off his lap and back on the couch and, in doing so, purposely knocked over her beer onto the spoo stain on Geronimo's shorts, thereby saving them both the agony of talking about it.

"I'm so sorry," Laura Ann said, jumping up to get Geronimo a paper towel and leaving Geronimo alone on the couch to think about what had just happened and how, if his teammates ever found out about his early ejaculation, he would finally have an officially sanctioned nickname. That nickname would be: Oops!

"Oops," Geronimo said out loud.

"What?" Laura Ann asked, sitting back down on the couch and handing him the paper towel.

"Nothing."

Laura Ann nodded and began to make small talk. "You're a football player, right?"

Geronimo delicately blotted his crotch and said: "Not too much of one."

"You graduating this year?"

"History teacher on my back," Geronimo said. "I'm *supposed* to graduate in December."

"Me too," Laura Ann said. "Come January, I'll be a middle school headshrinker in Beaufort."

"I don't know what I'll be," Geronimo said. "IPTAY ran out of gas and I've got mother problems, too. It's been a disappointing day."

"I see."

"It's been a disappointing *life*," he told Laura Ann.

Laura Ann eyed Geronimo for a second, and it seemed that she, like life, was disappointed in him. Then she put her bra and shirt back on and fiddled around some, throwing away beer bottles and stacking dishes, until it was clear to Geronimo that it was time for him to leave. So he left.

Geronimo's mother was waiting for him back at his room. It was first time she had ever been to campus to visit him. Their house in Florida was six hours away by car.

"Son."

"Momma."

"Where's your roommate?" his mother asked. Geronimo had no roommate, but he had once told her that he did. His roommate, Geronimo had told her, was from California, Nevada, somewhere, and they were the best of friends and sometimes engaged in impromptu drunken wrestling matches, which Geronimo let the roommate win.

"He's out," Geronimo said. "You come to apologize?"

"I came to do this," she said. She walked over to Geronimo and demanded his keys. He gave them to her. His mother then took the key to her house off the ring and returned the rest of his keys to her son.

"What'd you do *that* for?" Geronimo asked once he'd realized which key she'd taken. He was flat-out *pissed*, and felt like turning over a desk or a table, but he owned neither. There was just his mother, the couch she was sitting on, and himself. And you could not turn over yourself or your mother, could you? A mother was not a desk and her boy was not a table.

"I did it out of love."

"*Love.*"

"You need a job, friends, people," his mother said. "Not me and not that little bitty bike of yours."

"*Love,*" Geronimo repeated.

His mother sighed, rubbed her cheeks with her large, leathery hands. Geronimo thought his mother looked like some kind of fish, the way she moved her cheeks back and forth.

"You really gonna graduate next month?" she asked.

"Might."

"Might *what*?"

"Might fail history."

"Dale."

"I *know*."

"Come here," she said and walked toward the bathroom. He followed her. She turned on the light. They stood in front of the mirror together and she held up his hands, palms out. The hands were meaty and red and he felt very stupid just standing there, examining his fleshy mitts. So he made his left hand into the shape of Michigan, a state and a school that had not offered him a full scholarship.

"Your history teacher have hands like these?"

Geronimo admitted that his teacher did not. "He has dainty hands," Geronimo said.

"You know what to do," she said. "I'll see you at graduation."

His mother kissed him on the cheek and left him standing there, looking at the Michigan of his left hand. Michigan had not given him a full ride, but his hands were big and his teacher's were small, and that was something better than a state or a school.

The history professor was wearing gray sweatpants when he answered the door. His house was made entirely of stone, as in a fairy tale.

"Are Hansel and Gretel home?" Geronimo asked and then laughed and then thought better of it and scowled.

"They're both out, Mr. Geronimo," the teacher said, not smiling, not seeming especially superior or European, not wearing wire-rimmed glasses like Geronimo thought he would be. Geronimo pressed on.

"I want my C."

"Why?"

Geronimo held up his big hands.

"I didn't ask why I should *give* you a C," the teacher said. His hands were in the pockets of his sweatpants and he was flapping the pockets in a way that made Geronimo think of a parachute not opening all the way and the parachutist getting skewered by a tree. "I asked you why you *wanted* a C."

"What?" Geronimo asked, not quite getting it. "You think I'm not strong enough?" He punched his left palm with his right fist, making a wet *smack*.

"Come on in."

Geronimo came on in. The house was a disaster of books and blaring tv and beer cans and berber carpet. Geronimo had assumed that his teacher was married, probably to someone much better looking than the teacher himself. But now it was clear to Geronimo that his teacher lived alone and probably rented the house. The beer scattered around was cheap.

"You by yourself?" Geronimo asked.

The professor didn't answer. He sat down on the couch. Geronimo sat next to him. Two white men were playing ping-pong on the tv, moving quickly but stiffly, as if they were arthritic dervishes.

"It's the goddamned Olympic trials," the professor said. "I can't stop watching them." It occurred to Geronimo that his professor was drunk, and that now was the perfect time to plead his case.

"I want my C."

"Table tennis is an Olympic sport," the professor said. "Football is not."

"The world is broken."

"Fix it."

"I will. Give me my C."

"Why?"

Geronimo had an answer this time. "So I can graduate."

"Why would you want to do that?"

This was another question Geronimo had failed to anticipate. He gave the professor a panicked look. The professor handed Geronimo a Pabst from a cooler next to the couch and opened another one for himself.

"Let me guess. You want to graduate so you can get a job, for which you are not qualified."

"I'm qualified."

"No, you are not. Why did you come to this school in the first place?"

"Why?"

"Yes. Why did you want to play football?"

Geronimo paused for a moment. He thought the professor was looking for a profound answer and he wanted to give the professor one. But he could not think of anything except for the answer all his teammates would give, which Geronimo did not think was true in his case. But he gave it anyway.

"Coach said he would let me hit people."

"Fine. And have you hit people?"

"Not too many."

"Correct. So now there is no more football and you are only qualified to drink beer and let your body go to shit. Before you are graduated, you are allowed to do this; after you've graduated, you are not allowed. If you do what you're not allowed to, which you will, then you will end up alone." The professor made a circling gesture of the house with his beer, spilling some on Geronimo's head. The beer on his head caused Geronimo to feel as if he'd just woken from a dream.

"I understand, I do. I don't want to graduate. Please fail me."

"Alone, Mr. Geronimo. Get used to it. I don't care whether you want the grade or not. You will get your C. This is how the world works."

"I know it is," Geronimo said. He realized that the professor was right, and that he would be alone for the rest of his life and there was little he could do about it. Geronimo thought about hitting the professor, just reaching around with his right hand and slapping the professor on the right side of the head, directly above the ear. But even this, Geronimo suspected, would not make him feel any better.

"All alone," the professor said. He drank the rest of his beer, opened another one, and drank that beer, too. Then the professor got up and ran to the bathroom and began retching loudly, so loudly that he drowned out the sounds of the ping-pong match on TV.

Twenty minutes later the professor came back from the bathroom.

"You feel all right?"

"I feel good," the professor said, sitting back down on the couch and opening another beer. "Tomorrow I will feel bad."

"Tomorrow I'll feel *real* bad," Geronimo said, thinking about the abyss of his final game and the larger, more terrifying abyss that lay on the other side of it. "You sure you won't fail me?"

"Positive."

"Then what am I supposed to do?" Geronimo yelled. "Just tell me what I'm supposed to do!"

"Tomorrow we will feel bad, Mr. Geronimo. There is nothing we can do about it. Let us feel good tonight." With that, the professor offered him another beer and Geronimo took it.

It was halftime and Clemson was down three touchdowns and a safety to Florida State. After his talk with the professor, Geronimo was determined to make himself feel as good as possible during this, his last game, despite his ringing hangover. So Geronimo had sat on the bench for the first half and dispensed advice to the freshmen, many of whom actually played more than twice a game. Geronimo's advice to the freshmen was this: Don't even think about screaming like an Indian out there. The team's placekicker had tried it once during a kickoff the year before. Geronimo explained to the freshmen that the kicker, who had since graduated and gone on to the NFL, was from Slavia or somewhere and knew nothing about being on the warpath and didn't he have some balls to think that he *did* know something about it? So Geronimo had head-butted the kicker and then lectured him on his sole ownership of the kickoff whoop and war cry while the kicker was staggering around, trying to take off his helmet and get the bees out of his ears.

"What I do?" the kicker had asked once he'd removed his helmet and silenced the bees.

"There are no Indians in Slavia," Geronimo had told him.

"What?"

"I'm from fucking *Texas*," Geronimo had explained to the kicker, and he also explained this fact to the freshmen. This was not true, of course—Dale Lerner was actually from Florida, from the panhandle. But *Geronimo* was clearly from Texas, and being from Texas, thought that being from Texas explained everything that needed explaining.

"Understand?" he asked the freshmen. They did. The freshmen understood that they had played poorly, so poorly that Coach had sent them down to the end of the bench to be lectured about Indians and whooping and Texas and Slavia, which didn't even exist, they didn't think. It was a bad day for the freshmen.

And it was a bad day for everyone, including the baton twirlers. It was halftime, and the twirlers were out there on the field of play, throwing their shiny little sticks up toward heaven and then dropping them and distracting the marching band, who kept having to break step and avoid the batons, some of which were on fire. These miscues made Geronimo feel very good about himself indeed. One girl dropped three in a row and started crying right there *on the football field*. Dale might have sympathized with her crying on the field, but Geronimo did not suffer it.

So Geronimo sidled up next to one of the male cheerleaders, who was watching all this from the sideline.

"She's a disgrace out there," Geronimo told him.

"Janine's dropped a few," he admitted.

"An absolute disgrace."

"What are you doing out here?" the cheerleader asked. "Shouldn't you be back in the locker room?"

It was true. Geronimo should have been back in the locker room with the rest of the team, listening to Coach tell them how Florida State was tearing them a new asshole out there. This wasn't ex-actly Geronimo's favorite expression. To be true, Geronimo got extremely agitated just thinking about it. As he was standing there on the sideline, Geronimo kept whirling around, as if someone were sneaking up behind him. Geronimo could just *hear* Coach at that moment: Do you know that they are tearing you a new ass-hole out there? he would be saying back in the locker room. Then the coach would pause—he was a master of this sickening, foot-tapping, dramatic pause-and-stare number—until a majority of his teammates would admit that yes, they did know that Florida State was tearing them, etc.

All right, the coach would finally say. They are fucking you up the butt and you have said it yourselves. Now what are you going to *do* about it?

What Geronimo was going to do about it was stand on the side-line and not admit anything and bad-mouth the baton twirlers. Of course, he couldn't exactly tell all this to the male cheerleader, who was still standing there, waiting for an answer. In the olden days, everything would have been different and Geronimo could've told the cheerleader whatever the hell he wanted. In the olden days, you could accuse male cheerleaders of all sorts of offenses—homosex-uality, lassitude, piss-poor spirit—whether the cheerleaders were actually guilty of these things or not. But it was not the olden days anymore and Geronimo knew it, and so he kept his mouth shut.

"Well?" the male cheerleader said. "Are you going back to the locker room or aren't you?"

At the mere mention of the words *locker room*, Geronimo once again whirled around, giving the male cheerleader a good look at the name on the back of his jersey.

"*Lerner*, what are you *doing* out here?"

"Call me Geronimo."

"No."

Then the cheerleader did the same dramatic toe-tapping number that the coach did. What has happened here? Geronimo asked himself. Have our cheerleaders become our coaches? Have times changed that much?

So Geronimo, who was not wearing his helmet, head-butted the cheerleader. Just up and head-butted the cheerleader and let out this weak little dribbling war whoop. The whoop was so weak because the head-butting hurt, which it didn't when you were wearing a helmet. Geronimo closed his eyes so he didn't throw up from the pain. He wanted to throw up. He wanted to cry again, too. The pain was severe—sharp, nauseating electric volts shooting up toward his scalp, around his ears and down his neck.

When Geronimo opened his eyes, he was surprised to see the cheerleader sitting on the ground. The cheerleader didn't seem so much hurt as he was mad. He wasn't even rubbing his forehead; the cheerleader was just sitting there, glaring up at Geronimo. Geronimo recognized for the first time that the cheerleader was nearly as big as Geronimo himself, and that he might not take being knocked on his ass lightly. But still, the cheerleader *was on the ground* and Geronimo had put him there. He forgot all about crying. The olden days were back.

"What the hell was that for?" the cheerleader wanted to know from his position of sitting on the ground.

"That was for the olden days."

"What are you talking about?"

"I'm from fucking *Texas*," he said, and let out another whoop.

"I don't care where you're from, Lerner," the cheerleader said as he picked himself off the ground. "I'm not going to forget about this."

Geronimo didn't like the sound of that at all. But luckily, just then, his teammates came roaring out of the locker room. No one said anything about Geronimo not being in the locker room, and his teammates swept him along as they tore onto the field. Geronimo found himself whooping and beating on the freshmen's shoulder pads, and there was so much good feeling out there on the field that it was as if they were not twenty-three points behind; as if the cheerleader whom Geronimo had head-butted would not get up and exact his revenge; as if Geronimo himself had not been a scrub for four straight years and would not be alone for the rest of his life. Things became very clear for Geronimo. He knew that while he felt good at the moment, he would feel awful tomorrow, and would probably even regret the memory of all this good feeling. But so what? Because he was having his moment—the fans were on their feet, eighty thousand yahoos screaming for him, and they did not distinguish him from his teammates; as far as the crowd was concerned they were all the same steroided warriors happily beating on each other—and for that moment, it did not pain Geronimo that he was a final-game senior with no nickname except for the one he had given himself. It simply did not hurt.

The Fund-Raiser's Dance Card

The fund-raiser's name was Lee Ann Mercer and she wanted to go dancing. It was one of those late spring Friday nights where the wind was warm and wet and the air smelled like an overly chlorinated pool and everyone wanted to do something they hadn't in too long a time. The real estate agent and his wife turned off their television and went to get passed-out drunk at a bar with an outdoor patio. The too-young married couple with too many too-young children decided to hire a sitter and go see a movie that was not animated or a musical. The widower, who had practically *lived* in his bathrobe since his wife had died, put on a plaid blazer and a tie and said, "Let's *do* something," to no one in particular. And Lee Ann Mercer, who was hosting her annual fund-raising party for university alumni at her house at 107 Strawberry Lane, could hear music drifting from somewhere down the street and decided that she was going to go dancing.

Lee Ann stood holding a glass of white wine in the kitchen, next to the back door, and considered the implications of her impending departure. Her boss was in the house somewhere—chatting up all the wealthy white-haired men wearing tan bucks and linen jackets and their wives in their overly fancy yellow sundresses—and Lee Ann had the fleeting thought that he would resent her leaving her own party and thus violating the terms of her contract—not just as a hostess but as a university fund-raiser who was expected to put on and *stay put* at these kinds of functions. Plus, she was expecting someone in particular at the party: a thirty-nine-year-old alumnus from Raleigh, North Carolina, an ex–studio arts major and heir to his daddy's video poker fortune who lived by himself in a loft apartment with stacks of New York art magazines stretched well toward the ceiling and who regularly teased Lee Ann with promises of behemoth bequests to the university but thus far had not delivered. The last time Lee Ann had visited him—a month or so earlier—she had been in the middle of explaining his many gift options— named chairs, endowed annual exhibitions or installations, new goalposts—when the alumnus had kissed her, full on the mouth, and, to her surprise, she kissed him back, and wanted to do so again immediately after and now, too, even though he was a dilettante who left one too many buttons on his shirt unbuttoned and whose teeth were surprisingly crooked and jack-o'-lantern-like for a rich man. The alumnus—his name was Barry—had responded to her party invitation in writing, saying that he would come to the party and that he had a big surprise for her. Lee Ann did not want to miss his arrival. But no, Lee Ann quickly decided, she would not be missed: she would dance her way up and down the street, from house to house, and then slip back into her own house and no one would know the difference. "I haven't been dancing in *ages*," she told herself. Just then, she heard her boss's voice booming from somewhere in the house, and she quietly slipped out the back door, past her barking dogs, past the cigarette smokers. When the smokers asked where she was going, she rattled her glass and said, "Ice," then stepped out onto the street, and into the night.

On the street she stopped and listened for a moment. There *was* music playing from somewhere—Glenn Miller, Tommy Dorsey, someone with a big band from before she was born—and she did a happy little hip-shaking shuffle down the street as she mapped her route. First the Merrills', then the Yerinas', the Hammonds', the Cheevers', the Morriseys'; then, at the cul-de-sac, she would dance down the other side of the street: the Howards', the Charneys', the Lius', and finally the Parks' house, right across from her own. Lee Ann took in a deep breath. The air no longer smelled like chlorine but rather of sweet pesticide from the town's mobile bug fogger, but still the smell was chemical, and the sky was black and deep and it was the kind of night that made you feel very brave. Lee Ann had just seen a movie on the climbing of Mount Everest and so felt something of the adventurer in herself and she anticipated that she might, someday, tell stories about the night she danced her way up and down Strawberry Lane.

Lee Ann was not an impulsive woman, nor did she consider herself untrustworthy; but she wasn't above lying to herself on occasion, either. For instance, she lied to herself about her house all the time, and the lying did not trouble her much. Lee Ann lived in the house with two dogs and a husband. The house itself was fifteen years old and had white vinyl siding and black shutters and pillars that were not really pillars at all, but rather two thirty-foot strips of white-washed pine that stretched from front entrance to roof. They were not pillars, officially, because they didn't actually support the roof. "Those pillars couldn't hold up me *or* you," the contractor had told her when building the house.

"They're for decorative purposes," Lee Ann had said.

"Exactly," the contractor had agreed. "Those things don't do *shit*."

"Understood," Lee Ann had told him. Nonetheless, she called the strips of wood *pillars*, and she also referred to her home as being *lakefront property*, even though the lake was only a damned-up river and even though the water was so low that one had to muck through fifty feet of mucousy red clay before one got to the lake itself, which the EPA said was too dangerously polluted to swim in anyway, especially if you were pregnant. Lee Ann Mercer was not pregnant, but one of her dogs, a blockheaded black lab named Labbie, *had* gotten pregnant and had given birth to the second dog, a runtish black and gray mutt that Lee Ann had not bothered to name and refused to let in the house. The dog roamed and smelled like fish. When her neighbors complained about the mutt, who barked at night, all night, Lee Ann simply lied and said it was a stray, and that she couldn't take any responsibility for it.

So Lee Ann lied about her dog, and she also lied about her

husband, Teddy. Lee Ann's husband had paid for the building of the house when they had moved from Connecticut to South Carolina some fifteen years earlier, but he barely lived in it. He was the chair of the biology department at the university. Usually, when not stopping off at the house to nurse his broken heart or beg for Lee Ann's forgiveness or check his mail, he lived with one of his female graduate assistants. But for a while now, Lee Ann's husband had lived with the slutty manager of the bar he frequented and often, when drunk, talked of buying. He hadn't been home for several months. When neighbors asked about Teddy, Lee Ann merely said that he was busy at work but was otherwise fine, absolutely fine.

There was one more thing that Lee Ann lied about: her name. It was not really Lee Ann; it was Katherine. Katherine had taught fourth grade at a private elementary school in Stonington, Connecticut. Her husband's name was not Teddy but Ted. He'd taught biology at a private women's college in New London. Katherine and Ted were happy. They were! They were happiest when they walked the grounds of their highly mortgaged property and patted the Revolutionary-era stone walls and threw sticks for Labbie. The sticks were birch—no other kind of stick would do—and in her fourth grade class, Katherine taught her students how the Nipmuck Indians had made canoes out of birch bark and her students marveled at the native intelligence of the Indians. The descendants of those Indians were now supervising the slot machines a half hour away at the Foxwoods Casino, but Katherine did not mention this to her students, who were too young to appreciate how short the distance was from ingenuity to stupefaction.

But then Ted applied, interviewed for, and accepted a job at Clemson University in South Carolina. He did all of this without consulting Katherine first. "You'll get over it," Ted said when Katherine objected. Katherine simply stood there and glared at her husband. They had been married for six years, and this was the first time that her husband had said anything remotely like "You'll get over it." Katherine felt like she had been duped, conned into marrying the wrong man. "You'll get over it," she said and then spat on the ancient knotty pine floor of their bedroom, driving her husband from the room. Once he was gone, Katherine jammed her clothes into their suitcases and then spat on the suitcases, too.

Katherine became further enraged once they reached Clemson, because suddenly there were no more ancient, meandering stone walls and birch trees, and suddenly everything was air-conditioning and the Lost Cause and school fight songs and Jesus bumper stickers on jacked-up pickups with running boards, and suddenly being *Katherine* seemed unbearably *quaint,* hopelessly *obsolete.* So she tore the red bandana from around Labbie's neck and renamed herself Lee Ann.

She had gotten the name *Lee Ann* from a convenience store clerk at the Lil' Cricket. A week after she had arrived in Clemson, Katherine had gone to the Lil' Cricket to buy a loaf of wheat bread, which they did not have. She had to settle for Wonder Bread, which further enraged Katherine. She threw down the loaf on the counter and the clerk rang it up. Behind the clerk, there was a Xeroxed sign taped to the cigarette shelf that said: "I can only help one person at a time, and let me tell you, today ain't your day. (And tomorrow ain't looking too good, either)."

"Ain't that the truth," Katherine said, trying to be accommodating.

"No," the clerk said, "it *ain't.*"

Katherine didn't know whether the clerk had gotten her point of reference or not, but it didn't matter. What did matter was that the clerk was a tobacco-stinking, bleached-out bulge of a woman who wore too-tight denim shorts and a skimpy denim halter top with rhinestone studs and who *didn't take any shit.* The clerk's ID tag said *Lee Ann.* Katherine immediately knew she had to jettison her God-given name.

"Lee Ann," Katherine said, "I need to throw the baby out with the bath water."

"Lady, you need a job or somethin'," the real Lee Ann said, giving Katherine her change and her white bread and then ignoring her entirely.

So Katherine did what the Lil' Cricket clerk had suggested by word and by example: she got a job as a university fund-raiser and she changed her name to Lee Ann. Lee Ann had hopes that announcing her name change would do something to her husband, produce some sort of shock or regret, but when she told him over dinner, "I'm Lee Ann now," he merely smiled and said, "I know, I'm Teddy."

It was true: just like that, he was Teddy. Whereas before, as Ted, he'd been the kind of diligent, self-serious youngish man who ran 10K races for the cure—all cures—and ironed his chinos and made variations of the same healthy stir-fry meal three times a week, now he was Teddy: a slovenly, bearded, sport-sandaled, thriving middle-aged lothario who drank too much and bet large sums on college football games and told roaringly funny stories about his pickled brain and what stupid things that brain told him to do and overall Teddy was excellent company to everyone but his wife. Meanwhile, except for her job change, Lee Ann was much the same as Katherine, except older and much more permanently mired in regret and sorrow and loneliness. Lee Ann was the same as Katherine except there was more Lee Ann needed to forget. This was another reason she would go dancing.

The first house was the Merrills'. Wayne and Ellen Merrill were both history professors, both recovering alcoholics as well, and they were known for throwing parties where no booze was served but guests were encouraged to bring their own instruments—acoustic guitars, inevitably, and the rare squeeze box—for what the Merrills called "our famous after-dinner hootenanny." At one of these parties, Lee Ann had been cornered by Wayne Merrill who, armed with a twelve-string, had forced her to harmonize on a Glen Campbell song he insisted she knew but didn't and when the song—it was about the sorrows of drink—was over, Wayne had dropped his guitar and wept and asked Lee Ann if she knew how badly he wanted a drink right then? Lee Ann told him that she knew exactly what he was feeling and then fled the party and swore she would never go back, and remembering this, she considered skipping the

Merrills' house altogether in her quest to dance. But there were crashing sounds coming from the side yard, loud music that was recorded and electric, not live and acoustic. These were not the Merrills' sounds, and Lee Ann remembered that the Merrills were away in Europe on sabbatical and that they had rented the house out to some students. Lee Ann heard voices that were, in turn, seductive and violent, and these voices drew her, her feet moving her in an improvised two-step into the side yard.

The notable thing about the Merrills' side yard that night was that it was lit up like a football stadium. There were two garage floodlights going and four cars with their headlights on arranged around the perimeter. In the center of all this light were two ping-pong tables; on either end of the two ping-pong tables were two plastic cups of beer, and behind each cup—four to a table—was a man, or to be more precise, a boy. Each of the boys was wearing a golf visor and baggy shorts with many pockets and no shirt and flip-flops. They were playing a game, Lee Ann quickly understood, and the object of the game was to hit the ping-pong ball into the cup of beer. When this happened, the boy whose cup it was and his partner were obliged to chug their beer; the boy who'd sunk the ball and *his* partner were obliged, it seemed, to bump their fists or chests in celebration, whereupon they chugged their beer, too. Some of the beer spilled on the boys' chests and bellies during the chugging and even though some of the chests had hair on them and even though some of the bellies had already begun the outward bulge toward middle age, the effect of the light on the beer on the boys' torsos was like hot soapy water on Greek statuary.

Just then the song ended and a new one began and there was a great deal of whooping and suddenly Lee Ann was surrounded by the ping-pong players, who were dancing, and Lee Ann's first thought was, *revenge*. Because this, in a manner of speaking, was what Teddy had been doing to her for more than a decade now. There had been so many nights, at two in the morning, the hour when the bars closed, when Lee Ann lay in bed and imagined her husband desperately dancing through last call with his undergraduate lovers, his much younger sloppy bar managers, doing shots of tequila, admiring the happy wet sheen of liquor on a pretty-enough girl's upper lip. She imagined Teddy going to lick off that sheen and the girl not stopping him. It was the loneliest feeling imaginable, like writing thank-you notes from the bottom of a volcano. *Revenge*, Lee Ann thought again. Someone gave her a shot of something and she drank it and started dancing with the boys. It wasn't the kind of music she'd had in mind—not big band, but rather the famously tragic southern rock group with the famous three guitar attack—nor was it the kind of dancing she'd wanted to do—it was not couples dancing, but rather dancing in a circle, not so much moving your feet as stomping them. But still, it was music, and there was sex in it and in the dancing, too: there was sex in the way she took her long, blondish hair out of its complicated twists and knots; sex in the way she took off her light green sweater and tied it around her waist; sex, even, in the boys' air guitaring; sex especially when one of the boys—his visor was on backwards and upside down, his chest hairless– quit his air guitar and moved a little closer to her, as dancing partners should. Lee Ann had no fear that this was a pity dance: she was twenty years older than the boy, it was true, but she was still very pretty, she knew this, and while she had lines on her face they gave the impression of health and sun and not overage and while her clothes were mature they were not dated, nor were they designed to cover up her body's flaws, of which there were few. She and the boy circled around each other, dancing backward and then face-to-face, not touching, it was true, but to Lee Ann not touching was nearly as suggestive as the touching would have been.

"Is your name Ryan?" she shouted over the music.

"Yeah," he shouted back. He didn't ask how she knew his name—she had a theory that every other male born between Atlanta and Richmond between 1978 and 1981 was named Ryan—and in truth it didn't matter. What mattered was that Lee Ann had her Ryan and she was dancing with him and, for the first time in a long time, she felt good.

But then the song ended and the boys—her Ryan, too—went back to their ping-pong game and Lee Ann was left standing by herself, watching them. Was this what it was like for Teddy, too? Were twenty-year-old girls about adult sex in one minute and adolescent drinking games the next? Did Teddy wait around for them to change back? She was pretty sure he did, and for a moment she even felt a little sorry for him. In the shadows of the party, Lee Ann could see a line of girls, smoking cigarettes and glaring at her; they would wait for the ping-pong game to exhaust itself. Lee Ann knew this because once she had been one of them. Perhaps Katherine would have waited. But Lee Ann would not wait. She would not wait! That she would not wait seemed proof not of her desperation, but rather of her sense of perspective. There were other houses, other dance partners; there might even be a rich suitor with a suitcase full of cash waiting for Lee Ann back at her house. The point was, there was no point in dancing your way through the sweet, spring night if you did not give yourself over to its expansive mystery and promise. The ping-pong ball grazed one of the cups but did not go in and there was a great deal of arguing about the relevant Rules of the Game and in the midst of this, Lee Ann sneaked out of the party and continuing dancing down the street.

Had you seen Strawberry Lane that night from above, with the ability to see through roofs and walls and enclosed patios, you might have mistaken Lee Ann for a meandering drunk, for an attractive but troubled forty-four-year-old woman who had fallen off her medication. You would have seen her foxtrot into the Yerinas' house without knocking. The four Yerinas—mother, father, two adolescent girls—were sitting on the couch and watching a situation comedy about a rich family that had recently become a poor family. Both the Yerinas and their television counterparts seemed anesthetized and Lee danced around them to the show's theme song and exited through the back door without saying goodbye. There was no one home next door at the Hammonds', but the garage door was unlocked. There was a minivan in the garage and

Lee Ann slithered over the hood, climbed to the roof, and tap-danced on it as in a musical she'd once seen before moving on to the next house, Mr. Cheever's, where Lee Ann ripped the glass of gin out of the old widower's shaky hands, set it sweating onto the end table, twirled Mr. Cheever a time or two the way Ginger never did with Fred, then placed the glass of gin back in his hands, sat Mr. Cheever on his couch as a failsafe against the drink, the twirling, and waltzed out of the house, pausing at the bathroom to jiggle the handle so as to arrest the toilet's running. If you were watching all this from above, and if you were a certain kind of deity, you would have right then descended to earth, stopped Lee Ann before she entered her next house, and demanded to know if she were feeling all right, if something truly bad had happened to her to cause such behavior. Have your parents died? Has your husband left you? Are you lost and far from your true home? Are you stupid and blind with grief? And while it was true that Lee Ann's parents were dead (for nearly a decade now), her husband no longer really a husband, her home not exactly her home, they could not adequately explain her dancing. Does the mountain climber climb because he was beaten as a child? Does the sailor sail because he pissed his bed well into elementary school? "Let's not psychologize," Lee Ann would have said to the deity, "let's dance," making the deity whoosh up and away, back to his privileged perch, before she continued on to the Morriseys'.

As before, Lee Ann did not knock but walked right in the front door. Thom Morrisey was standing by himself in the living room, a cigarette over his right ear, a drink in his right hand, hair slicked back with either sweat or gel. He was dressed in a cream-colored summer suit and his tie was loosened as if he'd just returned from a nephew's wedding or graduation. When he saw Lee Ann, he looked back over his shoulder toward the empty room and yelled, "Oh good, the fund-raiser is here."

"Will you please fix that fuse," a woman yelled from inside the house, and it was only then that Lee Ann noticed that the house was dark except for the light coming in off the street. Then, after a moment, the woman asked, "*Who's* here?"

"The fund-raiser."

"Which one?"

"The Yankee fund-raiser," Thom said, then took the cigarette out from the crook of his ear, then began patting himself for a light.

Immediately, Lee Ann's dancing felt diminished, demeaned, the way the mountain must be by the mountaineer's athlete's foot, the ocean by the sailor's urinating over the bow. Apparently, even if you danced your way up and down your street, you could not forget that you were a fund-raiser, that people expected you to ask for things they did not exactly want to give. And if you were from Connecticut, then you could not forget that you were a Yankee, even if South Carolina had become no less your home than Connecticut ever had been, even if you tried to explain that people and places are not that different, and that folks in Connecticut hated black people and loved NASCAR, too. And if you were the wife of a wayward husband, your dancing could not help you forget that the world was choked full with cheating hearts—because Thom, who was an alum and was assistant dean of admissions, was married to Bette, one of Lee Ann's few friends, and Lee Ann knew that Bette was in Charleston, visiting her Alzheimered mother, and that the woman yelling from somewhere in the house was not Thom's wife.

But still, Lee Ann could see no other choice but to dance. Besides, perhaps this was a necessary obstacle. True, she'd always disliked Thom, who could be trusted to be somehow both dull and offensive, who inevitably would tell familiar racist jokes and then, when someone objected, hold up his hands in mock defensiveness and say, "What? What?" Perhaps this was a necessary sacrifice if she was to continue her journey up and down Strawberry Lane. Perhaps you had to dance with a sleezeball peckerwood before you could move on to better things.

"Let's dance," Lee Ann said.

Thom stopped patting himself and smirked at Lee Ann. "I always *thought* there was something going on between us." He held up his glass. "I need a refill. Be right back."

"You don't need a drink," Lee Ann said.

"Don't move," Thom said.

The minute Thom was out of sight, Lee Ann moved, tiptoed first in the direction of the kitchen, where Thom was making his drink and humming, then off toward the right, toward where the woman's voice had come from. The house was one of those deceptively large and meandering ranch houses, and so Lee Ann walked down a three-step flight of stairs, up another one, through a rec room, past two bathrooms, and into a sunroom—a small, entirely glassed-in room furnished with a love seat and an end table. By the time Lee Ann arrived at the room, it felt as though she were in a different house altogether. But it was the same house, and there was the woman sitting on the couch, knees tucked up to her chest. She was younger than Lee Ann, but not much younger; she was pretty, but not any prettier than Bette, Thom's wife. Her blonde hair had been overpermed or bleached over the years and looked tired. Her blue eyes were red, as if she'd been crying, but she wasn't crying just then. She and Lee Ann looked at each for a while, and then the woman said, "The power went out. I hate the dark." When Lee Ann didn't respond, the woman said, "I don't know what I'm doing here, do you know what I mean?"

"You're fucking my friend's husband," Lee Ann said.

"I know," the woman said. "Why am I here?"

Lee Ann held out her arms to the woman, and the woman rose and took her arms as the submissive partner might, and they danced. It was a very controlled dance, because of the tight quarters, but it seemed important to Lee Ann that they not leave the tiny sunroom: this was the space they were given and this was the space they would use. It was the first time she'd ever danced with another woman like this. It did not feel good or bad. It did not feel erotic, nor did it feel odd or repulsive. It felt like dancing with oneself and once the dance was over, Lee Ann almost asked the woman if she'd like to come with her as she finished her dance up and down Strawberry Lane. But then she heard Thom yelling from somewhere, deep or shallow, inside the house, "Where are you? *Hey*!" Lee Ann turned her head in the direction of the yelling and then turned back to the woman. She was back on the love seat, her knees tucked up to her chest again. Lee Ann would not wait for her bare-chested, visored, ping-ponging Ryan, but this woman would wait for Thom, that was what she was there for. So Lee Ann left her to wait.

A word on Lee Ann as a fund-raiser: she was good. She could sweet-talk an alumnus into buying a thousand-dollar commemorative plaque in a second. Her fellow fund-raisers would have been jeal-ous of Lee Ann's success if they hadn't been so completely cynical about their work. When talking to potential donors on the phone, Lee Ann's colleagues made clownish, mocking gestures with their lips and their hands. When they actually did browbeat an alumnus or parent or corporation into making a pledge, they called the dona-tors "suckers" and their donations "blood money." She wasn't like them, nor was she like her boss, an alumnus himself, an ex-second-string defensive lineman who liked to talk about his work in terms of *client* and *contract*.

"When you give money to the school," he told his prospective *clients* and his new employees during orientation, "you are not simply handing over money to the school. Rather, you are signing a *contract* for success with the school itself. And as we all know," and here Lee Ann's boss looked at his clients and employees knowingly, eyes wide open so as to ward off the temptation to wink, "you cannot honorably break a contract."

The potential donors were inevitably lawyers, CPAs, industrial managers, and so on the whole were very skeptical about *gifts*; but they were absolute devotees of *contracts*, and so this tactic rarely failed. But Lee Ann found it unnecessary hoo-ha. All she did was ask people for money; if they said no, she asked someone else. Lee Ann gave the overall impression of not caring whether an alumnus gave money to their alma mater or not, which people, of course, found attractive, and they gave to such a degree that Lee Ann was the school's top fund-raiser, more proficient, even, than her boss, with his *contracts* and *clients*.

Which was why Lee Ann was so baffled by Barry, the video poker heir from Raleigh. It wasn't that he'd yet to give her and the university his money, wasn't that he said No to her. Lee Ann could take No. In fact, she found No definitive and comforting. But Barry wouldn't say No, not Yes, either. He said Maybe, had said it a dozen times over the past four years, had said it so many times it produced something like a feeling of longing in Lee Ann. A longing for what, exactly, she did not know, but she did know that longing was one of the things to be afraid of in this world. Longing was the enemy. It made you want something you did not really want as badly as the longing suggested you did, and which, if you got, would not make you happy. You could *want* but you could not be *satisfied*. Lee Ann had even tried to use her boss's *clients* and *contracts* business on Barry, but he had been a studio arts major, after all, and had no idea what she was talking about. Which made her long for him, or his money, or both, even more. Perhaps this was why she had returned his kiss; perhaps this was why she was thinking of him now. Lee Ann was at the very arc of Strawberry Lane's cul-de-sac; she could have easily turned and watched her house, watched to see if Barry— he drove a Alfa Romeo, the only one, he insisted, in the entire state of South Carolina—had arrived yet. But she didn't; because this was what dancing was for. It could not make you forget the longing, but it could transform it. Lee Ann remembered watching her parents dance at her and Ted's wedding; they were good, dullish, ordinary people, but they were great dancers. When they were not dancing, Lee Ann forgot about them; but when her parents were dancing, Lee Ann wanted to be them. *This* was what dancing could do.

And this was what it did do, because when Lee Ann reached the Howards' house, the door opened without her even touching the knob. The Howard family—Terry, Alison, their son, Ian—was standing there in the doorway, as if arranged for a picture. Terry was sitting in a wheelchair, and he said, "We've been watching you dancing."

"What the hell—" Lee Ann began, and then, mysteriously, felt an overwhelming need for privacy. She hustled herself inside the house, then closed the door behind her.

"What the hell happened to you?" Lee Ann asked.

Terry didn't say anything; he just sat there in his wheelchair. His hands were in his lap; he was wearing the gloves worn only by golfers or baseball players or the wheelchair bound. But Alison said, "You've got to be kidding me."

"Sure I am," Lee Ann said, even though she wasn't, even though she had no idea what had happened to Terry. This was clearly something she should have known: because it was a small town, because Terry lived on her short cul-de-saced street, because she should have known that something bad had happened to him. Even if she were wrapped up in her own longing and her own sorrow, Lee Ann should have been at least aware enough to know what had put her neighbor in a wheelchair. After all, she saw him every day, at dusk, riding his bike up and down Clemson's hilly streets, the hilly streets without any shoulders to speak of, the hilly shoulderless streets on which the students drove too fast too drunk. But Lee Ann worked at the university; she would have known if a student had put Terry in a wheelchair, because it might have been something she might have had to mention in reassuring potential donors that the school wasn't allowing all of its students to get drunk and slaughter Clemson's citizen population wholesale. So it wasn't a student, but they weren't the only ones driving on Clemson's hilly, shoulderless streets. There were also the retirees, the legions of retirees, and it wasn't just that the streets were hilly and shoulderless but that they were without center lines, too, and so even if you weren't a retiree who shouldn't have been driving because you were going a little blind and even if your reaction time weren't a little dulled by your eighty-odd-year history of reacting, then it would be difficult to tell exactly where you were on the road—whether you were too far over or not over far enough—until your right fender clipped the rear wheel of the bicyclist in front of you, sending him over the ditch and headfirst into a pine tree, shattering the helmet that was supposed to save not just his life but also his spinal column, his fine china delicate vertebrae.

"I'm so sorry," Lee Ann said.

"Thank you," Terry said.

"It happened six weeks ago," Alison said. "So yeah, thanks."

"Alison," Terry said. "Quit it."

"At least Teddy came by," Alison said. "He brought a bottle of good gin."

And there it was, on the dining room table; Lee Ann could see it. It hadn't been opened. It was good gin, better than what Teddy himself drank. And apparently Teddy was a good, generous person, better than Lee Ann herself was. Ian, Alison and Terry's son, still hadn't said anything. He was looking away from Lee Ann, toward the wall, and she followed his eyes and saw that there were a dozen holes in the plaster, fist holes, and that they were both at wheelchair height and higher. Her eyes went back to Ian, whose own eyes were hollow and pitted and looked much like the fist holes he was still staring at. He was a teenager, she saw, a normal teenager except sadder, which is to say he was the saddest person she had ever seen.

"I'm not supposed to drink," Terry said. "But would you like some gin?"

Lee Ann didn't say anything. She didn't move. She had forgotten all about dancing; she couldn't remember how she'd gotten to the Howards' house, had forgotten even entering the door and closing it behind her. Outside the house there might have be longing and its opposite, but inside there was only shame and fear, which you might be able to dance away if only they didn't stop you from dancing in the first place.

"Anyway," Alison said, "we were watching you dancing . . ."

"It was very beautiful," Terry said. "Very impressive."

"And we were wondering—" Alison said.

They were wondering if she would dance with one of them. And she had to: her husband had brought them gin—weeks ago, probably—and she owed them at least a dance. But with whom? She wouldn't dance with Terry: she had seen people dance with the wheelchaired, at weddings, parties, and the dancing reeked so much of pity that it couldn't be called dancing, the people doing it couldn't even be called people. And she wouldn't dance with

Alison—because Alison hated her, hated most everyone, including her own husband, maybe her own son, and because what they'd be doing would not be dancing but would instead be something closer to war.

"Come here, you," Lee Ann said to Ian.

He came to her, even though he would not look at her. Terry wheeled over to the stereo, pressed a button or two, and music came out of the speakers. It was one of those popular Duke Ellington songs that people who don't listen to music listen to when they want to listen to music. Lee Ann and Ian danced to it anyway. They danced as befitted their circumstances: stiffly, awkwardly, as though their legs were in polio braces, as though they were *both* teenagers and not just one of them. Lee Ann could dance better than this, of course—there was the time when Ted and she danced at their wedding on the heels of a dozen lessons devoted to that once dance, and their two-step had wowed their guests, if not themselves—and she wasn't trying to dance awkwardly, but she did, and it seemed to her the most genuine thing she had ever done. It was the most surprising moment of her life: she was capable of doing something genuine again; or maybe it was the first time she had ever done something genuine. And just as she was trying to remember if she'd ever done anything genuine before this moment, Ian moved his hand from her back up to the back of her head, which he cupped gently for the remainder of the song—the song that began with her doing something for him, ended with him doing something for her.

"We'll all be fine," Ian whispered in her ear. "Please don't cry." But she didn't know what he was talking about, she wasn't crying, she was certain of it, even though her eyes were blurry and her voice shook and cracked as she said, "Goodnight, take care, I'll see you soon," and then backed out the door.

Outside, something was on fire. Lee Ann could smell the smoke, feel the fingers of heat. Lee Ann was glad that something was on fire; it distracted her from the Howards. Something was on fire! Perhaps it was her house; perhaps it was her! It wasn't the Charneys' house or the Lius', she saw this as she danced past them, the smell and the heat getting stronger as she got nearer the Parks' house. She could actually see the flames now, their own shadowy dance with the magnolia and white pines. The Parks' house was on fire! It was a happy prospect—not because she didn't like the Parks, but because theirs was the last house before hers, and it seemed a suitably big note on which to end her dancing: one final, pagan dance around the fire before going home to her guests, her clients, her Barry, and all their past, present, and future contracts.

But the Parks' house wasn't on fire at all. Lee Ann saw this as she danced closer, saw that the fire was coming from somewhere off to the right and behind the house. She followed the flames until she came to, in the middle of the Parks' backyard, a bonfire. In the middle of the bonfire, Lee Ann could see the white-hot skeletal remains of wooden pallets, a recliner, a dresser even. There were a dozen or so people sitting around the fire on a variety of wooden chairs and Lee Ann suspected that those chairs would also be in the fire before too long. The people around the fire were completely quiet, as if ruminating on the fate of their seats.

"What is that *smell*?" someone asked. Lee Ann couldn't see his face, couldn't see anyone's face.

"Fish," someone said. "Who threw a fucking fish in the fire?"

It wasn't a fish, it was Lee Ann's nameless dog; Lee Ann could see it sprinting around the perimeter of the firelight, could smell it orbiting them.

"It's not a fish," Lee Ann said. "It's a dog."

"Who is that?"

"It's Katherine," Lee Ann said, because the fire, her dog, her dancing, the night had suddenly made her extraordinarily tired—tired of being Lee Ann, tired of owning a dog she didn't really own and didn't even know its name or gender.

"Hello, Katherine," another voice said. "It's Ted."

Lee Ann walked over to the voice. It was her husband, all right. He was wearing a Hawaiian shirt open to midchest; Lee Ann could see the swell of his belly, on which rested his hands, one of which cupped a cigarette; his beard was enormous and red in the firelight. Even his head looked huge; there was a long-billed fishing cap perched on the very peak of his skull, and it was clearly pushed down as far as it could go; there were angry waves of hair pouring from underneath it. Lee Ann couldn't remember the last time she'd seen him, but since whenever that was, it looked as though her husband had swallowed his former self.

"I'm so tired," Lee Ann said. "Can I have your seat?"

"Do I have to move first?"

"No," Lee Ann said, and plopped down on his lap. She did this so suddenly that Teddy jerked his cigarette away and dropped it to the grass; Lee Ann could see it glowing down by her feet, next to a beer can that Teddy picked up and took a pull from. There was no difference between how the beer smelled and how Teddy smelled. Lee Ann wiggled around until she was properly settled. It felt as though she was sitting on an inner tube that had not yet lost its middle.

"Well," Teddy said.

"I was just at the Howards'," Lee Ann said. "Just horrible."

"I know," he said. "I gave them a bottle of gin."

"That was nice of you."

"It was actually your gin," Teddy said. "I took it from the liquor cabinet sometime back."

"Oh," Lee Ann said.

"You don't like gin," Teddy said. "Not really."

"That's true."

Someone across the fire stood up, threw the chair on which he'd been sitting into the fire, threw a beer can in the direction of the dog, whose fish stink was still whizzing around the fire.

"What's going on here?" Lee Ann asked.

"Roger and Lucy are getting a divorce," Teddy said.

"So you're burning their furniture?"

"It seemed like a good idea at the time."

"Was it Roger's idea or Lucy's?"

"Possibly neither," Teddy said, and waved vaguely in the direction of the house, which was completely dark. Lee Ann had been there many times—for dinner parties, to watch the World Series, to celebrate this or that. But at that moment it was hard to believe that anyone had ever lived there.

"What were you doing at the Howards'?" Teddy asked.

"Dancing," Lee Ann said.

"I don't want a divorce," Teddy said suddenly.

Lee Ann nodded. "Me neither."

"Why not?"

"I've never liked you better," Lee Ann said. It was the truth. She had lied to herself for years about how Teddy had wrecked her life; she had longed for the time when she was Katherine and he Ted. But the truth was that she hadn't ever really liked Ted—he was officious, he was dull, but he was good, so it was difficult to actually justify or understand her dislike for him. But Teddy was easy to dislike, it was understandable why she would hate him, which made her, in turn, like him. Love no longer applied, if it ever had; sex was irrelevant, too (there was no stirring in her sitting on Teddy's lap, even though she could feel a stirring in him). But she liked him now, she couldn't deny it, and couldn't imagine her life without him, couldn't imagine him not coming home for months at a time even though he was never more than a few miles from home, couldn't imagine him not running around on her with girls half his age, making a happy debauched spectacle of himself all over town. If he kept on the way he was going—which he would—then Teddy would almost certainly die before she did, and this made her sad. Losing Teddy would be like losing one of the poles, North or South. The thought made her sad, and it made her even more sad to see him here, near despondent, watching the flames of someone else's marriage, when he should be out there, doing the things he did so well.

"There's a big party down at the Merrills'," Lee Ann said. "They're playing beer ping-pong."

"Beer pong?"

"Right," Lee Ann said. "Plus girls."

"Okay," he said. "I love you. But do you mind if I get up?"

She didn't; they both stood up. He kissed her lightly on the cheek, and without another word he left the bonfire. The other men got up and followed along, as did the dog, its smell trailing behind it. Lee Ann was alone again. She had heard other women—women who had never married, divorced women, widowers—say that they liked being alone. Lee Ann didn't believe this for a second. They were lying, she was certain of it, and this was another thing to guard against: not loneliness, which was inevitable, but lying about it. A car door slammed in the distance. It was a tinny slam, not the door of a truck but of a sports car. It was probably Barry. Perhaps he would give his gift to her tonight; perhaps not. Perhaps he would give her more than his gift. Perhaps whatever he gave her would make her less lonely for a little, but the loneliness would come back, it had to, there was no sense lying about it, and there was no sense in longing for a time when she wasn't lonely. And while she was at it, there was no sense in lying about the dancing, either. It did not make her less lonely, less likely to long. It was simply a way of getting from one place to another, and now she needed to get back home, to her party, where people were waiting for her.

The Hotel Utica

I t was the year of divorce, of murder in the alley behind the theater and late-night knocks on the door, and it was also the year when grand old hotels were reopening in all the dying, shuttered downtowns of the industrial East Coast cities after which the hotels had been named. For years, the hotels had been used not as hotels but as flophouses, soup kitchens, Catholic outreach headquarters, and federally funded drug counseling and needle distribution centers, if they were used for anything at all. In each building the upper-story windows had been bricked over and there were drop ceilings everywhere and the intricate tile lobby floors were yellowed and cracked and smelled, somehow, of the rotten teeth they couldn't help but remind you of. But then there was a war, which we assumed we had won and was popular, and an economic upswing followed and within months of each other the Hotels Springfield, Worcester, Bridgeport, Providence, Lowell, Concord, Manchester, Albany, Syracuse, Rochester, Buffalo, and Utica all were purchased, rehabbed, and opened for business. The assumption seemed to be that if the hotels were restored to their former splendor then people would come.

People came, mostly forty-eight-year-old men. Most of these men were former residents of Syracuse or Manchester, etc., who had moved south or west around the time when the hotels had fallen into such total disrepair. The men who ate and stayed at these hotels soon quit their jobs in digital this or computer that—jobs that had made them rich, quick, and allowed them to send their children to private colleges without the need of scholarships—and moved back to their native cities with their wives in tow and became consultants of one sort or another and struck up a loose affiliation with other returned exiles to other cities. Soon, these former exiles formed an organization called Prodigal Sons and published a guidebook and set up a Web site devoted to what night was piano jazz night at the Hotel Worcester and what room at the Hotel Buffalo was said to be haunted by which doomed Roaring Twenties billionaire. The *New York Times* even ran an article about the trend and made bold predictions about what it might indicate about the national mood, and this is how I heard about the Hotel Utica reopening in the first place.

It is perhaps interesting to note that after my wife and I had moved from Utica—our hometown, where we met in high school some twenty-five years ago and fell in love—we lived in Gainesville, Florida; Raleigh, North Carolina; Tuscaloosa, Alabama; Tucson, Arizona; Durango, Colorado; and Clemson, South Carolina, and in each place you could have the *New York Times* delivered to your home and in no place did this make us any more or less happy than if we had been forced to go to the store to buy it or to read a different newspaper altogether. But it was in Clemson—where I was working as the university fund-raiser I've for twenty years been, and where Sarah Beth was the fourth grade teacher she swears she won't always be—where I read about the Hotel Utica.

"What do you think of when I say 'the Hotel Utica'?" I asked Sarah Beth.

"Unfortunately, I think of you," she said. We were sitting at the kitchen table. Our two boys were in their bedroom, arguing in their high, sweet voices about the most effective way to slaughter fire ants. Outside our huge A-frame window bamboo shoots were swaying in the breeze. Shafts of sunlight were making flickering geometric designs on our new shag carpeting. It was pretty by almost anyone's standards. Sarah Beth wasn't exactly happy with me. The night before we'd gone to a dinner party that was called a supper club, the difference being, apparently, that at a supper club the hosts decided on the theme and disseminated the menu and each guest was responsible for bringing an item on that menu. The hosts that night were the Bishops and the theme was German and we brought a strudel and Scott Bishop answered the door wearing nothing but a Speedo and leather sandals, and by the end of the evening things had gotten out of hand and I said a few things I shouldn't have about the Speedo and how it was more than enough to cover up what Scott Bishop—who taught computer science at the college and was no bigger a peckerwood than your average citizen— didn't have, and now it was the next morning and Sarah Beth was still thinking about the friendships I'd probably ruined. I could tell this by the violent, snapping way she folded and unfolded the newspaper. When she looked at me her blue-black eyes seemed to want laser beams to shoot out of them. This wasn't the first time something like this had happened, but it wasn't any worse than in Tuscaloosa when a group of Sarah Beth's fellow teachers and their husbands took us to eat at a restaurant where Jefferson Davis was supposed to have dined. I asked for proof of this, because there are seventy-five restaurants in Alabama and Jefferson Davis apparently ate at all of them, and when the owner/hostess showed me a grainy, yellowed picture of Jefferson Davis (it could have been him; I didn't and still don't have any idea what he actually looks like) sitting at the very table at which I was sitting, I said, "*That's* not Jefferson Davis," over and over until some of the husbands took off their Sputnik-sized class rings and started cracking their knuckles and Sarah Beth made me wait in the car.

"When I think of the Hotel Utica," I said, "I think of snow, perfect virgin white snow that you can't ruin even when you drive on it and I also think of marble columns and bellhops wearing top hats and an orchestra playing somewhere."

"What are you talking about?" she asked. I showed her the *Times* article and she read it, her face growing harder and harder, and by the time Sarah Beth finished reading her face looked much like the sinister granite gargoyles on the façade of the Hotel Utica that I was already getting moony about. I could picture everything already: the polished walnut bar; the art deco mosaics on the thirty-foot-high lobby ceiling; the enormous gilt smoky mirror behind the bar; the tiny, elegant, intricately carved tables you couldn't sit at comfortably if you were the oversized modern man so many of us have become; the gaudy, low-hanging beaded crystal chandeliers: the women in evening gowns bathed in all the soft light from those chandeliers; the men, handsome and understated in their gray wool suits. Gray wool suits! What troubled heart couldn't be eased by putting on a gray wool suit?

Obviously, the *Times* article had a different effect on Sarah Beth, because when she was finished reading it, she flung the newspaper back at me and said, "I'll divorce you if you make us move again."

When Sarah Beth said this, she was maybe thinking of the time when I made us move from Tuscaloosa to Tucson and ended up drinking tequila in the truck with the Mexican movers, who as it turns out weren't really movers or Mexicans, but that's another unfortunate story. Me, I was thinking about the last time I'd been in the Hotel Utica. This was at lunch with Sarah Beth and my mother. My father had died too young of a heart attack a month or two earlier, and Sarah Beth and I—not yet married a year—took comfort in each other, but who did my mother have to take comfort in? So after my father died, Sarah Beth and I ate lunch twice a week at the Hotel Utica with my mother out of duty and pity. We were all eating heavily mayonnaised egg salad sandwiches on white bread, which was the only thing edible at the Hotel Utica at that time. The place was mostly empty, the lone remaining business on an especially gutted block, and everything—the city, the block, the restaurant—smelled like wet fur on charred wood. Visitors refused to believe there hadn't been a riot sometime in the recent past. It was April and snowing hard and icy against the windows and sidewalks, and the snow only added a glaze of failure to the dirty, dark snow piles on both sides of Genessee Street. There were black people everywhere and my mother—who had grown up in the neighborhood when it was Irish, had gone to Our Lady of Mercy High School right around the corner, and had learned a thing or two in English class about figurative language and misdirection—complained bitterly about the "nigger snow." The fifth time she used the phrase, Sarah Beth threw down her napkin and went to the bathroom. My mother and I sat there quietly—whatever there was to say had been said and ignored many times over already—and watched a black man wearing a parka with a fake fur–lined hood piss against the side of the Hotel Utica. A king menthol dangled precariously from his mouth. When he was done he waved to us and then—for our benefit, I suppose—tried to stick the cigarette in his fly, but the zipper must have been broken because he couldn't get the cigarette to stay and it kept falling to the sidewalk. I was certain that the black man would try this thing with the cigarette and his fly a few more times, then put the cigarette back in his mouth and be on his way. Once the man was out of sight I was certain that my mother would start hissing like a punctured tire. Once my mother started hissing I was certain that I would be confused about whether I should align myself with her or the black man. I was certain all of this would happen, and when it did, it became clear to me that I was certain about too much, about all the wrong things.

"Mother, Sarah Beth and I are moving to Gainesville, Florida," I said, just like that.

Right then, Sarah Beth returned to the table. She hadn't heard my announcement, and so looked mighty confused when my mother said, "Your father and I went to Florida once, on vacation. He sweated constantly. He was always in need of a dry shirt. Natives were selling things in paper sacks out of the trunks of their cars. They said there were peanuts in the sacks, hot boiled peanuts, but we'd never heard of such a thing and didn't believe them. I got a chancre sore, which cracked and bled at awkward moments. The only houses were bungalows, and when I asked your father what kind of name 'bungalow' was, he said, 'It's a made-up name.' 'Why in the world would anyone want to live in a house with a made-up name?' I asked him. And then we left and never went back."

But to return to Clemson, South Carolina, where because I was who I was I insisted that we move again—back home to Utica, this time; and because Sarah Beth was who she was she said, "That's it, I've *had* it, we're getting a divorce"; and because South Carolina divorce laws are what they are, we got a divorce within a week, with no hassle and no time to have smart second thoughts; and because the heart wants what the heart wants, Sarah Beth and our two boys stayed in our house in Clemson and I moved back to upstate New York, into a top-floor room at the Hotel Utica.

Was there sadness on my part? Yes, there was sadness, but there was also relief and gratitude that we'd ended it right then, before I made all of us even more miserable. Because this was not the first time we'd argued, and Sarah Beth herself had said many times that my restlessness made everyone unhappy and was like a disease, and there was no palmetto tree or desert cactus lovely enough as far as I was concerned and the weather was always too hot and much overrated and the people too dull or too clever and there were always too many T-shirt shops and the state liquor laws were either too strict or not strict enough, and it was true that we had moved too much and our boys had had to change schools and make new friends too many times. So perhaps things were better this way; this was what I told myself and I also told myself to keep busy, which is what people tell themselves when they don't want to wonder whether they've done the right thing or not.

So during the day I started working as a fundraiser for Utica College—the same job I'd left over twenty years earlier. At night, I wrote an advice column for *Prodigal Sons* magazine, which was just one of the dozens of new men's magazines with more or less naked women on the covers that somehow weren't considered porno-graphic magazines, maybe because they contained advice columns like mine. And speaking of my advice column, it was called "The Heart Wants What the Heart Wants," which became something of a personal motto and which I often repeated to myself while sitting alone in my·well-appointed, wainscoted, shabbily genteel room at the Hotel Utica. My room overlooked Genessee Street, which was no longer gutted and abandoned, but instead had been tricked out with new gas streetlights and populated with antique stores, art galleries, and microbreweries. The refurbished Stanley Theater once again booked plays that had been big hits in Manhattan only two years before. It was difficult to get a seat anywhere and the chamber of commerce couldn't say enough about how important the pedestrian traffic was.

Like everyone else, I did my fair share of strolling up and down Genessee Street at night (which my parents never allowed me to do as a teenager because they were convinced I'd be murdered with a switchblade, a kind of knife I don't think they'd ever seen and may not have ever existed outside the movies). But mostly, I just sat in the Hotel Utica bar and wrote my column. To "Haunted in Hattiesburg," I said that I understood what it was remember the big Victorian home in which you'd been raised being broken up into too many apartments, to remember the downtown department store where your grandfather had taken you to see the Christmas train exhibit every year boarded up with its roof fallen in, to remember the movie theater where you'd once seen John Wayne fire that gun and ride that horse become a wig shop that kept highly irregular hours, to remember all these things and be so haunted by them that you had to move away and never ever come back. I wrote to "Alienated in Atlanta" and "Alienated in Austin" and "Alienated in Anaheim," and I told them that I, too, knew what it was to move from place to place, from warmer climate to drier climate to warmer climate again, looking for a place you could honestly call home and in no place finding that home and finally wondering—to yourself, never to anyone else—whether the problem wasn't with the places, but with you. To "Pariah in Pensacola," I said I knew all too well that this kind of alienation could lead a good man to do bad things, like the time I helped Sarah Beth chaperone her fourth grade class trip to the North Carolina Capitol building, and one of her students said that her daddy had voted for Jesse Helms ten times, and I said that I didn't realize that they let mongoloids vote in North Carolina, and everything was fine until one of the smart kids defined "mongoloids" and the girl began to cry. I empathized with "Scarred in Savannah," who told me what it was like to watch his hometown go to shit and then be convinced, deep down, that everyone or thing or place he touched would eventually go to shit, too. To "Conflicted in Carmel," I agreed that it was possible to love a city and hate what it had become, just as it was possible that you could love your parents and hate the thought that you might become them, that you might become something worse than them.

My mother was still alive during the year that Sarah Beth and I were divorced and I moved into the Hotel Utica. In fact, we ate lunch there once a week. She was seventy-nine years old and lived in a nursing home that was called an assisted living condominium and used a cane or walker, depending upon her mood, but otherwise seemed much the same as she'd been twenty-odd years earlier. She wasn't much impressed with the new Hotel Utica, and while she couldn't express her distaste for black people anymore (they had disappeared from the neighborhood entirely, a phenomenon that no one, not even the newspapers, commented upon) she was convinced that there were homosexuals everywhere and the word "fag" was never far from her lips. To distract her from this kind of libel, I would gesture to the beautiful, gleaming restaurant of the Hotel Utica and the overflowing, prosperous-looking lunch crowd and say, "Doesn't this remind you of when you and Dad used to come here?"

"We never came here," she said.

"You didn't?"

"Well, maybe once or twice. But it was nothing like this."

"How was it different?" I asked, because the economy was still booming, money kept pouring in from somewhere and everywhere, and the owners of the Hotel Utica were committed to restoring the place to what it had once been, never mind the cost, and I knew they'd want to know if something wasn't quite right.

"For one, there weren't so many fags drinking fancy drinks before," she said, and then pointed at my Manhattan.

"This is a Manhattan," I told her. "Dad used to drink these all the time."

"Your father drank nothing but beer," my mother said. "Fort Schuyler beer that was so cheap he could afford to drink himself to death by the time he was fifty-five."

"I think you're remembering him wrong," I told my mother, although I was having a difficult time remembering him myself. The only thing I could remember clearly about my father was that he once showed me how to change the oil in my car, and what this taught me was not how to change the oil in my car (I forgot how immediately), but that my father was a more capable and therefore better father and person than I could ever hope to be. I said to my mother, "I remember Dad drinking Manhattans, two every night, and he had a heart attack because they run in his family."

"When are you going back to South Carolina?" my mother asked me, because to save myself some grief I had lied and told my mother that I was simply in Utica on extended business, and that everything with Sarah Beth and the boys was fine.

"Why don't I take you back to your condo?" I said. "I've got plenty of work to catch up on."

And I did have plenty of work to catch up on, dozens and dozens of letters yet to answer for my advice column. To "Content in Concord," I concurred that nothing made you forget your troubles quicker than sitting in your hometown's handsome hotel bar and drinking a drink—a Gibson or a Manhattan or a Rob Roy—that your father and grandfather might have drank and not smoking the cigars featured prominently in maple humidors but happy, at least, to have them around for authenticity's sake. To "Soul Searching in Springfield," I expressed my encouragement and agreed that while the Hotel Springfield's in-house swing band couldn't make you entirely forget that you'd called the boy next door a "spic" right when the neighborhood was turning from Italian to Puerto Rican— while the in-house swing band couldn't quite help you forget what you'd said and the kind of person you were, you could listen to an optimistic Tommy Dorsey tune and marvel at how the hotel and the city had changed for the better and perhaps you had, too. And in my pre-Thanksgiving column, I described how the snow was falling gently, so gently, outside my window, and how people in scarves and overcoats were shopping on Genessee Street, and how there wasn't a broken or boarded-up window to be seen and how, for the first time in a long time, I felt like something wasn't horribly and irreversibly wrong with me and with the world. "Have a happy holiday," I told my readers. "Be thankful. All is well."

And all *was* well, until someone was murdered in the alley behind the Stanley Theater. It was Arnold Mills, who with his wife had lived in a room across the hall from me. His body was found by one of the stagehands after a performance of *Evita*. Arnold hadn't been stabbed, which my parents once feared would be my fate; instead, someone had strangled him with his own white cashmere opera scarf. It had been an especially clear, frigid night, and Arnold's impressive handlebar mustache was thick with ice when the stagehand found him. The police guessed from the stiffness of his limbs and the thickness of the ice on his mustache that Arnold had been dead for at least one act.

Arnold's death cast a shadow over the Hotel Utica—he was well liked and could always be counted on for cocktails and a game of bridge or pitch on a lonely Sunday night—but it wasn't much of a shadow, because after all these kinds of things happen in any city, no matter how safe, and besides, the police assured everyone in the neighborhood that there was nothing to worry about, and that they would soon find the killer.

Then two other strange things happened. One, the police discovered during their investigation that Arnold's wife, Ellen, had left him a week before he was murdered, and in fact was in their old home in Asheville, North Carolina, the very night he'd been strangled in the alley. The two of them had never made much noise in their room, and no one at the hotel had known Ellen had left Arnold, or even that they'd been having problems.

The second strange thing that happened was that someone began knocking on my door in the middle of the night. The first time it happened was a week after the murder, three days after it was revealed that Arnold's wife had left him. It was two in the morning. I was in a deep sleep and heard the knocking as one will, faintly, the knocking at first part of my sleep and then slowly pulling me out of it. It didn't alarm me much. I simply got out of bed and opened the door. There was no one there. The hall light was too bright and it made the red carpet look worn, and so I closed the door and went back to sleep.

The next night it happened again. This time, I woke up all at once and found myself ten feet away from my bed, crouched down behind the door, holding a fire poker with both hands. My head hurt and I was breathing hard. The night before, I'd thought nothing of who'd done the knocking; this time, I thought too much, and was convinced it was Arnold's murderer coming for me. I was so full of this kind of terrible middle-of-the-night logic that I said, loud enough for someone in the hall to hear, "I know who you are." Then, choking up on the poker with my right hand, I flung open the door with my left, absolutely prepared to brain whomever I found in the hallway.

There was no one in the hallway. I closed the door, but this time I couldn't go back to sleep. In fact, I sat in my desk chair in my boxer shorts, fire poker at the ready. It was just before four in the morning. I could hear newspaper delivery trucks pulling out of the *Observer-Dispatch* parking lot to make their morning deliveries. As a fund-raiser, I often had to get up early to go to an alumni breakfast fund-raiser four hours away, and the delivery trucks reminded me of getting in your car before you're really awake and the streetlights glinting off the wet streets (the streets never seem to be dry in the too-early morning) and driving without realizing you're driving and the heat in your car just beginning to work and you have four hours to go and you feel somewhere between loneliness and belonging and you wish you'd just be in one place or the other and soon the sun comes up cold and weak the way the sun finally came up that morning over the *Observer-Dispatch* building on Genessee Street.

At lunch that day I sat in my usual spot near the piano, warily eyeing my fellow diners, thinking that in all likelihood the murderer and door knocker was among them. But none of them looked like murderers; in fact, all of the men (there were mostly men in the restaurant) looked as baggy-eyed and pale as I knew I looked. Stan Vincent, who'd moved with his wife Ann from Las Cruces, New Mexico, into the Hotel Utica four months earlier, was so exhausted that he kept falling asleep while waiting for his mock turtle soup to be served. So I got up, walked over to his table, sat down next to him, and said, "Has someone been knocking on your door in the middle of the night, too?"

"What?" he said, snapping awake.

"You look exhausted."

"I've been up all week, begging Ann not to leave me and go back to Las Cruces." He rubbed his eyes with his fists, and then removed his hands and opened his eyes, which were wide and startled, as if Stan couldn't believe the eyes were his.

"Why does she want to go back there?"

"Because she was happy there," Stan said. "That's why Arnold's wife left *him*, because she'd been happy in Asheville and he made her move back to this hotel and dress up every night for dinner and she was sick of it. When Ann heard about it, she realized she was sick of it, too. She's upstairs packing her bags right now."

"I'm sorry," I said.

"It's been happening to a lot of the guys," he said, and then fell back asleep again, chin tucked snugly into his blue blazer.

So that was why everyone looked so tired at lunch, but it didn't explain why someone was knocking at my door in the middle of the night and it didn't explain why the knocking continued for the next three weeks. I stayed up, hoping I would catch whomever it was, thinking about who it possibly could be. Arnold's murderer, that was still a possibility; but it also could have been one of the guys who stayed at the hotel, one of the guys whose wife had left him and out of grief he had gotten drunk at the bar and mistaken my room for his. Or it could have been one of the waiters, disgruntled that I had given him a bad tip. When I wasn't theorizing about who was doing the knocking, I was terribly lonely and afraid, sitting there in the dark, and so, naturally, started thinking about Sarah Beth and the boys. It was the middle of December, around the time when John always got awful, raging ear infections and I hoped the antibiotics were working this time. Peter was always terrible around the holidays and could be counted on to harass his mother about getting him the right Christmas presents (unlike the previous Christmas) and I hoped he was cutting her a break this time. And I remembered Sarah Beth and the time when I had seen one too many alumni back for homecoming give me a "gator growl" and I said to one yahoo dressed all in orange, "Gators don't growl" and started throwing rocks at the alligators in the University of Florida's main pond to prove my point. I was caught by university police, fined, and sent home, where I had my first inkling that something was wrong with me, and began crying, hard, the way you do when you don't know you want to cry until you've actually started. In between sobs I told Sarah Beth I couldn't live in Gainesville anymore, it didn't feel like home, and Sarah Beth ran her fingers through my hair and said, "That's all right, it's fine, we'll go wherever you want." And in thinking about Sarah Beth and the boys, I felt something between warmth and wistfulness, which of course is the perfect state in which to fell asleep. And so I did, which was when the knocking on the door would recommence. Each night, I'd jump out of the few minutes of sleep I'd managed to get, only to find that bright, sad hallway empty, once again.

And then, out of the blurry days and nights of not sleeping, I was back having lunch with my mother again. I'd lived in the Hotel Utica for nearly a year at this point. Arnold's murder hadn't been solved, but there was other, more widespread trouble by this point. There'd been talk of the economy faltering—*Prodigal Sons*, for instance, started publishing monthly and the girls they picked for their covers were more naked but less famous—and so the City of Utica had pumped even more money into the downtown as part of its stimulus package and at night the streets were still bathed with light, but the light was dim and sad and there seemed to be a general feeling that something truly bad was going to happen.

As I said, we were at lunch, and as usual my mother was muttering the words "fag" or "queer" every five minutes or so, until finally I said, "Mother, what are you talking about?"

"*Look*," she said, and for a moment I thought if I turned my head I would see the black man from twenty years ago pissing against the wall, then trying to stick his cigarette in his fly. But I turned my head and looked and saw nothing out of the ordinary, just people here and there eating lunch.

"I don't see anything," I said.

"They're all men," my mother said. I looked again, and it was true: the restaurant was full of barely conscious, amnesiac men eating by themselves. I knew and had talked with many of them: Larry, who'd returned from Richmond, Michael, who'd returned from Sarasota, etc. There were all heterosexual, as far and I knew, and after several Gibsons or Manhattans they couldn't stop talking about their estranged wives and how much they did or did not miss them, and it was as painful and predictable to listen to them make their excuses as it is to listen to oneself.

"They're all men," I said. "So what?"

"*Fags*," my mother said, loudly. At the word all the other men looked up sharply and guiltily—as if someone had shouted "murderer" or "door knocker" or "husband" or "father" or "wanderer" or "dreamer"—before returning their attention to their newspapers and their bowls of soup.

My mother is now dead and there was another war—also popular but much scarier—and it caused an economic downturn, and the Hotel Utica has gone the way of all the other hotels except for the Hotel Worcester (who knows why these things happen?) and the Prodigal Sons and their magazine are no more and Arnold Mills's murderer, as far as I know, was never caught, but Sarah Beth and I are remarried, and all thanks go to Sarah Beth's eighty-year-old mother, who, like so many women of her age, fell and broke her hip in the Wal-Mart parking lot. She fell in early December, not too long after Arnold Mills was killed. I didn't know about Sarah Beth's mother at the time, and I also didn't know that Sarah Beth and the boys had come to Utica to attend to her and had been there for nearly a month.

Anyway, it was the night before Christmas, around eight o'clock, and I hadn't slept for more than an hour on a given night for more than three weeks. I stood at the window and looked at Genessee Street. Just as I'd imagined on that fateful day back in Clemson, it was snowing that night, big dense flakes flying and settling everywhere, and as a matter of fact the snow was perfect, as white and lovely and church-quiet as snow gets and not at all ruined by people driving on it. Downstairs in the hotel bar there was a jazz trio playing and not an orchestra, because the jazz trio was cheaper and the owners were cutting back, but still, it was cheerful and soothing, and I wished that Sarah Beth were there to see it and hear it, and I thought how I'd never see her or the boys again and that instead of a family I now had a lonely hotel room and a strange knock on the door every night, which was exactly what I deserved, and sated from all this monstrous self-pity I fell fast asleep.

I wasn't asleep for more than five minutes when someone knocked on the door. I broke out of sleep and I ran to the door (I forgot to pick up my fire poker this time), screaming, "I'll do whatever you want! Please! Don't leave!"

It was Sarah Beth, of course, standing in the hallway. She looked brilliant and godlike in all that bright light. It could have been her knocking on my door for the previous days and weeks (Sarah Beth has since told me that she'd been in town taking care of her mother for approximately the duration of the knocking), but I haven't asked her outright, and it doesn't really matter who it was, and it doesn't matter where we live now, either. All that matters was that I looked at Sarah Beth in the doorway and felt exactly as I had in Tuscaloosa, Tucson, etc., which is to say I felt like a husband and father who was mostly happy and somewhat disgruntled and alienated, and the idea that I would feel totally happy if I lived in the right place seemed as quaint and silly as the hotel room in which I was staying and the gray wool suit draped over my desk chair. And so I said to Sarah Beth, "I've missed you. I made a terrible mistake. Please don't leave. I'll do whatever what you want."

"It's Christmas Eve," she said. "Let's go home."

And then Sarah Beth took me by the hand and I let her lead me out of the Hotel Utica and toward home, wherever she decided home would be.